ABOUT THE AUTHOR

Fish Boy is Chloe Daykin's first novel, which she
wrote while studying for her MA in Creative Writing
at Newcastle University. It won the Northern
Writers Award, is longlisted for the UKLA Book
Awards, and has already garnered critical acclaim.
An artist, designer, playwright and teacher, Chloe
lives in Northumberland with her husband and two
boys. She is currently working on her second book,
The Boy Who Hit Play.

ABOUT THE ILLUSTRATOR

Richard Jones is an illustrator based in Devon with
more than twenty years experience in the creative
arts. He enjoys walking the dog and swimming in
rivers. Richard has also illustrated picture books,
including *Feelings* and *The Snow Lion* and is now writing
his own books.

First published in 2017
by Faber & Faber Limited
Bloomsbury House
74–77 Great Russell Street
London, WC1B 3DA
This paperback edition first published in 2018

Typeset by Faber
Printed by CPI Group (UK) Ltd, Croydon CR0 4YY

A CIP record for this book is available from the British Library

ISBN 978–0–571–32676–1

2 4 6 8 10 9 7 5 3 1

CHLOE DAYKIN

Illustrated by Richard Jones

ff

FABER & FABER

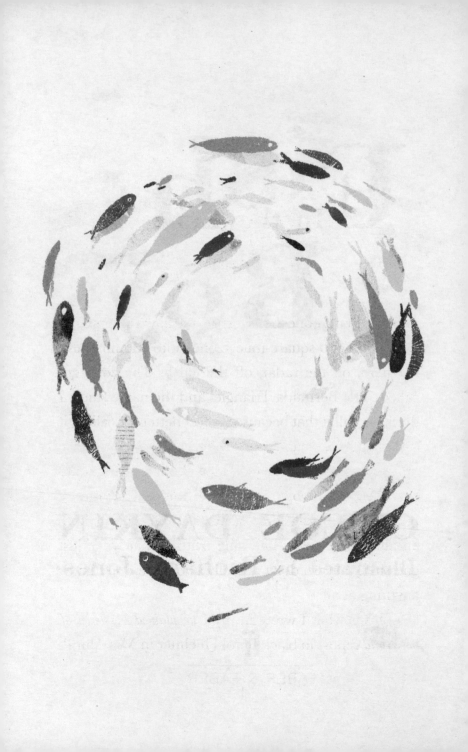

In the Zone

Since 1914 over one thousand people have disappeared in a 500,000-square-mile zone into nothingness, nowhere, off the radar, off the earth. The zone got called 'The Bermuda Triangle' and the name stuck. I think we call it that because we feel better for calling it something. Like names make us feel in control, like we understand stuff we have no idea about at all. It could be called the Goopatron or the Shidozzle Pyramid. It could be a black hole, a portal to another galaxy, an alien force field. The only truth is that we're just guessing, that we don't actually know, we don't know anything at all.

This is what I wrote in my *Unexplained Mysteries of the World* report in black Berol Fineliner in Mrs Ahira's humanities class at 2.24 p.m. And this is what I'm thinking right now, in the sea, when a *THING* swims up to my face, blows bubbles into my Vista clear mask goggles and says . . .

Kezdodik

Kezdodik
Kezdodik

Run

What do you do if you find a talking *THING*?

You leave it and run.

And then you feel bad and come back.

But then it's gone and you don't know if it was real at all, or if maybe you imagined it?

And now you're standing on the beach and there's no one else around. The sun's going down and your towel's gone missing, and your clothes and your new Nikes. Maybe Jamie Watts took them – or maybe it was the *THING*. All these questions make your head hurt. You want to run back into the sea to make them go away cos the water's like a plunger on your head and sucks them out, like carbon dioxide into trees. But you can't because tea'll be ready, cos the sun's gone and it's Sunday, which means pie and chips night and who would want to miss that?

I'm Billy Shiel and these are my questions cos this is me. Right here, right now, on Stepson beach. You can see me through the cliff railings. I'm the one with the goosebumps. The speck on the sand with the blue trunks. People call me Fish Boy. My skin goes up and down like the waves. My mind goes in and out like the sea. They say I've always got my mouth open, but what's wrong with that? Did I say they call me Fish Boy? Ha ha that's just a joke. Actually fish have really good memories, even goldfish. They can remember sounds for up to five months. You can train a fish to swim back to you for its dinner, from upriver, from the sea. You just play the sound and it comes right back like a boomerang.

So now I've got to run, before my chips get cold, up the cliff path, past Zadie Eccleston from class 7RH's house, through the hawthorn hedge with spikes like razors, over the 'Look Out For Frogs' sign and into the back door like the wind, like lightning, like the fastest no-shoes-and-practically-naked boy you've ever seen.

Hover

I'm in the kitchen in exactly eight minutes twenty-seven seconds. My second best without-shoes-on time. I can tell cos of my National Geographic watch, which is accurate above and below water up to ten metres. Dad's standing at the table looking at me in my blue trunks.

'You know the rules,' he says.

'But the chips, Dad?'

'No trunks at the table.'

'Can I just put them in the oven?'

'What, the trunks?'

'The chips.'

'Right, I mean no. I mean get a towel.' He's already got the sauce on his. He's picked his knife and fork up.

He's on a hover. I wish I was on a hover. I'm not even on a sit down. I'm on a drip and shiver.

'What about a tea towel?'

'I'm not having your never-you-mind on my tea towel.' Dad takes a pride in his tea towels. He gets them for his birthday, for Christmas. His favourite one says 'I'm too sexy for this tea towel'. It's hung up in the kitchen, next to the one from the Heavy Horse Centre that says 'Keep calm and eat cupcakes'.

'Where's your clothes?' he says.

'I don't know.'

'Where's your shoes?'

'I don't know.'

He looks at me right in the eyes.

'Where's Mum?' I say.

'In bed.'

'Again?'

He looks away. 'I'll get your dressing gown, son,' he says and ruffles my hair. He goes upstairs and gets my grey fleecy one. I've got three dressing gowns but the grey one is my favourite. I'm twelve and it's actually size thirteen to fourteen but I like the way the extra length covers my hands. Sarah Collins says that fleece is really made from plastic bags and I wonder how plastic bags can be so cosy. I can feel the heat prickling down my arms. Fleece is the best, it's like putting on a radiator.

Dad makes me a little table, with a knee tray. We eat the chips and pies. They've gone a bit cold. Neither of us says anything. I eat mine like Sir David Attenborough, award-winning broadcaster and naturalist. Everyone loves Sir David. He's the best. He knows what needs to be known. He's asked all the questions and got all the answers. He knows what to be scared of and what not to be, when to get in the water and when to get out. My fork ducks under the pastry like it's going into a bat cave, through the rock crack, into the cathedral chamber, like it's exploring for the first time. The bats fly out and away. My fork becomes the red-tailed hawk, my knife the prairie falcon.

From a chopper David shouts against the wind: 'The hawk needs all of its aerobatic skills and powers of concentration to snatch one of the confusing multitude.' I prepare for the kill. 'Don't play with your food, son,' Dad says.

'I'm not playing, I'm exploring.'

'If you discover any meat, let me know.'

I think, if my fork finds a piece of steak first no one will ever know about the *THING* and it'll all be okay and Jamie Watts will give me my Nikes back. In my head I ask Sir David what he thinks and he whispers in his dead calm voice, 'And now the female is leaving the nest.' He's always switched on to nature is David. He's a professional.

Fingers of Steel,
Strength of a Bear

So now here I am and here is Jamie Watts. I didn't think I had anything in common with Jamie. Not even shoe size.

Now I know I do.

He's standing in the school yard with Archie Longdon and Oscar Pierce. They're doing keepy-uppy with Archie's Man-U ball by the electricity hub. The sign by Jamie's head says 'DANGER: RISK OF DEATH'. There's a picture of someone falling backwards, a big stabby arrow poking him. If there was a speech bubble it would say 'aaaargh', but there isn't. He's just falling down and down into nothing. Jamie looks up. I feel my breakfast move in my stomach.

'Nice shoes, man,' Jamie says. I look down at my old lace-up gym shoes, my toes pressing up against the ends. I look at Jamie. He's wearing my Nikes. My mouth opens but there's no sound coming out. It's dried up like a rock pool in the sun.

Oscar laughs and does something I can't see behind my head.

'Nice one,' says Archie.

Jamie kicks the wall. I watch the ends of my Nikes get scuffed. I hate scuffs. I think, what would David Attenborough do? What would David Attenborough do? Sir David wouldn't jump off the boat with his diving gear on into this. He'd send down a camera on a stick. Or he'd just give the nod to start the engines and get out of here. In my mind I ask him and he says, 'The lead male in a pack may attack at any moment,' and bumps off over the Serengeti in a Land Rover.

So I turn and walk away. I picture the yard as a seabed, my body in fish mode. I wish I was a mackerel. Mackerel have excellent communication and move-as-one skills. They're the socialites of the deep. Unless you're from a different shoal and then they might eat you. If I was a mackerel I'd be looking for a kelp forest, so that's what I do. I go for safe ground, move into the shadows. What I find is Becky Ramsden showing everyone a YouTube video on her iPhone of a cat driving a JCB. She's in the middle of the watching gang. I duck under and in between and people say 'ow' and 'oi' and 'sod off' but I get right next to Becky and that's when I hear them.

'Can anyone smell that?'

It's Jamie.

'What?'

Archie.

'It smells like . . .'

And Oscar.

'Fish fingers.'

'Fish brain.'

'Fish Boy.'

They're across the yard, circling us. I look around and think this is not a kelp forest, it's a fish swarm, a bait ball. This is how dolphins get mackerel. They put us in a cyclone. They go round and round, turning us tighter and tighter. Then they burst through with their mouths open and shearwaters dive at us from the air with cormorants and gannets. It's a feeding frenzy and we're in the middle. We're the bait, the prey, a sitting target. That's when Archie's PE bag with a water bottle in flies up and on to my head. That's what makes me fall on the ground. Jamie Watts charges through everyone and they all scatter. It's just me and him and he sticks the Nike on my chest and comes right close up to my face and says, 'Don't you like my shoes, Billy, don't yer?'

I'm lying there waiting for the bell, for Mrs Curtis on morning duty, for Jamie's jaws to open and swallow me. I close my eyes and wait, but nothing comes. I open them and see him going backwards. He looks all weird and he can't move his arms or legs. There's a finger on his neck, another pressing into his shoulder.

'Leave him alone,' says the voice behind the fingers. It's a small voice. They let go and Jamie drops and backs off. I see a new kid standing there in a blue checked puffa jacket and dark-rimmed glasses. He's shorter than me, shorter than anyone else in the yard.

'I'm against violence,' he says and offers me a finger, his best right-hand middle. I pull myself up off the ground. I think his finger will pop out of its socket, but it doesn't.

'I'm Billy Shiel,' I say. 'People call me Fish Boy. My skin goes up and down like the waves. My mind goes in and out like the sea.'

'I'm Patrick Green,' he says. 'Fingers like steel, strength of a bear.'

'Brown, black, polar or koala?' Technically koalas

aren't bears and although people think they're very cuddly they're actually quite vicious.

'Technically koalas aren't bears,' he says and our eyes meet. 'Grizzly,' he growls. His growl is less impressive than his mighty hands. He holds one out and I look at the fingers of steel. I imagine them crushing mine. He sees me looking and puts them away. We shake thumbs. Even his thumb feels superpowered.

I see the blood flowing back under my nail. It goes from white to pink again. I look at Patrick Green and think where did you come from? I think about comings and goings and timings and life. I think of tribes and herds and straggly ones catching up from taking too long at the water hole, caribou and swallows crossing continents just to be at the right place at the right time. But I don't think about it for too long because the bell goes.

Brains Look
After Themselves

Me and Patrick hang around together for the rest of the day. It turns out he came from Crystal Palace. Before that County Armagh, Bloomington Minnesota and the Kyle of Lochalsh. 'Dad's work demands flexibility,' he says.

Jamie Watts doesn't bother us at all. When Becky and Sheree walk by, Patrick flexes his fingers at them and they walk away, laughing. They must get a buzz out of this cos they come past four times at lunch break.

At last break I show Patrick my place behind the fall wall. It's at the side of the field where the grass meets the stone and goes up in concrete levels. We call it the fall wall because pretty much most days someone falls off it. Sometimes deliberately, often not. Zak Wyming tried a parkour butterfly-kick once and it went wrong. He slid off head first on to the concrete and landed kind of wonky. He ended up with a broken rib and the nickname Zonky. He also missed out on the trip to the birthplace of the Venerable Bede, which was actually pretty good. I'm sure Mr Royston the caretaker has to clean extra hard around the fall wall or there'd be red bloody concrete all along the bottom of it.

We pull up on to the wall and shuffle back enough so we don't fall off, but not so far back that we soak water off the grass and into our trousers and look like we've wet ourselves.

'Pick a number between one and four,' Patrick says.

'That's a small range.' I shrug. 'Shouldn't it be between one and ten?'

'No.'

'Why?'

'Just pick one.'

'Okay.' I think hard. 'Three.'

He rolls up his left sleeve. *I knew you would pick three* is written on his wrist. It has smudged a little under the shirt.

'Nice,' I say and lean over to double-check it

actually does say three. It does. I wonder why I look like a number three sort of person. Does everyone think that about me? Do cooler people pick four, or one?

'Shake my hand,' he says. I do and when I open mine it is full of red spongy balls. 'Magic circle,' he says and taps his nose.

'You brought balls on your first day?' I say. I think of my collection of grey stuff I picked out before I started here. Grey pencil case, grey bag, grey folder. No labels, no designs, nothing stand-outable, nothing noticeable at all. Till I got the Nikes.

I hand him the balls back and check no one is looking.

'Yeah,' he says and shrugs.

Becky and Sheree walk past again and laugh. Zadie Eccleston's hair comes round the corner, followed by Zadie. She tucks some of it behind an ear. The wind blows it back out. The sun shines on her vampire rucksack.

When we were little, me and Zadie used to drive a red and yellow plastic Tiny Tikes car up and down our street. Together. Every day. We used to do loads of stuff together. Not now though. She moved round the corner and we started here and it just sort of stopped.

She walks off past the science window. Her skin is brown and shiny in the sun. Mine turns the same colour as the red spongy balls. I don't know why this happens, just that sometimes it does, mainly when I wish it wouldn't, which is always.

I don't tell Patrick about the *THING*. I don't tell anyone. In humanities Mrs Ahira draws a diagram of the water cycle and writes 'Water's Incredible Journey' in blue marker. I think about Mum in bed, about my Nikes, about the *THING*. I look out of the window and see its face coming up to mine.

Kezdodik

Kezdodik

Kezdodik

'Billy?' Mrs Ahira looks at me. I have no idea what the question was.

'Um . . .' I say and go red again.

The bell buzzes and I try to sneak out but she calls me over. 'How's the report going?' My *Unexplained Mysteries of the Universe* report is now officially a week overdue.

'Okay,' I say.

'Okay?'

'It needs some work.'

'Right,' she says and tilts her head forwards. Her eyebrows go up. Last week her and Dad *discussed* it. And me. And us. 'I'm here if you need anything, you know,' she says. I know she doesn't mean the coloured paper or spare Berol Fineliners sort of anything, although I do like those. I like the smell when you take the lid off. 'If you ever want to talk . . .' She stops piling up papers on her desk.

I don't. 'Okay,' I say, moving towards the door like a Minecraft Creeper. 'Bye.'

I run out to catch up with Patrick. His mum comes to pick him up with his little sister. She's wearing a pink Mummy's Little Angel sweatshirt and screaming her head off. 'A bit far from the Arctic, aren't you?' I say and point at the car. It's a white Volkswagen Fox. 'Ha ha, white fox, get it?' His mum looks at me but doesn't laugh. She's sitting behind the wheel in a white shirt and blue trousers with a line up the middle. Her hair is very curly but not moving. If you turned her upside down her head would be great at cleaning pans. She stares out the windscreen and rubs her hand across her forehead, which is sweating. I look at Patrick but he's making jelly beans pop out of his ears for his sister.

She stops crying and sticks one up her nose. I walk home on my own.

*

I take the key out from under the juggling gnome on the top step and go upstairs. I've got good at going up quietly lately. The secret is socks and speed. I can move so slow you wouldn't know I was there. It's great for stairs and wildlife watching. Stairs is easier though cos you don't have to worry about the angle of the sun and what kind of shadow you're making and where it falls. If you're at the wrong place at the wrong time your shadow moves before you do. Then you're done for. There's no light on the stairs unless you put one on, which I don't.

At the top I see the door's open a bit. I push it just enough to slide through sideways. The light inside's really bright. It's like that by the sea – you always get more of everything. More light, more air, more wind, more rain, more storms. It's full on, extreme. It lets itself go wild.

I see the shape of her in bed. Her breath makes the sheets go up and down. I step over the magazines on the floor that say 'Luxe for less' and 'Love your body'. Dad has drawn beards and googly eyes on all the models.

19

Mum's eyes are closed. A cloud moves across the sun. I see the shadow go over her face. 'Hi, Billy,' she says. This makes me jump cos her eyes are still shut. Her voice sounds like she's using lots of effort to make it come out. 'Wanna come in?' She pulls the duvet back. It's white with daisies sewn on. We bought it together at Tesco. When we got home she was dead disappointed cos the daisies were only on the bit you could see in the packet and it made you think they were going to be all over, but they weren't. I put my bag down, step over the socks and pants and stuff on the floor and climb on top.

'Had a good day?' she says and opens her eyes a bit, tries to smile.

'We had science.'

'You like science.'

'I like nature.'

'Righto.' She puts her arm up and I tuck in and lie on her shoulder.

I look up and see her eyes are closed again. 'We had a debate.'

'About science?'

'Microbes. Mrs Jones says I've got a very lively mind.'

'Fancy a biscuit?' She points to the Hobnobs packet

behind the picture frame. It's the photo of us all at Alton Towers on the log flume. Dad looks properly terrified. I get us one each. We eat the Hobnobs and look out of the window at the sea, the line of it at the bottom of the sky. Not that it stops there in real life, just that's as far as we can see. If we could see the whole thing it'd be too much. It'd fry our brains. It's like the way we can't imagine infinity, the way space just goes on and on for ever. Brains look after themselves, they sort out what we can cope with.

The front door goes and I hear Dad's voice and someone else's. They're coming up the stairs. We look at each other, brush the crumbs off the duvet. Mum props herself up on a pillow. Dad opens the door and I see it's Dr Winsall.

'Hello, young Billy,' he says.

I just stare at him.

'Want to go watch a bit of telly, son?' Dad says.

'Not really,' I say. Dad gives me a look. Mum kisses me on the head.

'Go on, love,' she says.

I climb out of bed and wait at the top of the stairs and do my best silent listening.

I think of Sir David in the dark, in the Gobi Desert of Mongolia with the long-eared jerboa. It scurries about, blind. Totally reliant on sound. Its ears are massive, longer than any animal. David whispers, 'His hearing is so acute he can even detect sleeping insects.' The jerboa hears an owl and jumps a mile.

Dad sticks his head round the door. I jump clean off the carpet.

'TV's downstairs last I saw,' he says and ruffles my hair. 'Here, I got you this.' He pulls an actual Twix out of his pocket and winks. I look at the shiny gold wrapper and go downstairs feeling very un-shiny. I put *The Blue Planet* DVD on and watch the bit where the seal goes up the beach. A killer whale comes after the seal but it turns round and barks in its face and keeps going. It doesn't let itself get dead or eaten or anything. It just keeps going.

Bigger and Blacker

That night I have this dream. I'm on the beach, but it isn't really the beach cos there's cactuses. You have to watch where you're walking cos of the spikes and I've got bare feet. I'm trying to get to the sea, but it keeps getting further and further away. The closer I get, the further away it goes. Then there's this cave and Jamie Watts is standing by it. Sir David is nowhere to be seen.

'Catch a load of this, Billy,' he says. 'It's a beauty.' He's pointing in the cave. I can't see in cos it's too dark. The cave gets bigger and blacker, like it's a mouth opening up, like's it's not a cave at all.

The cave mouth keeps coming at me, stretching out, like all the pointy rocks are teeth. The cactuses all get closer and higher. I have to put my arms over my head so they don't scratch. I put my hands over my ears.

'Don't yer like it,' Jamie Watts says. 'Don't yer?'

I try to run, but there's an ice-cream van blocking the way. It puts a cone in my hand and scoops chocolate chip on top of toffee fudge and strawberry cheesecake and bubble gum and crunchy mint. I can't hold on to it all. I'm just about to drop it when the ice-cream man sticks his head out right up close to my face and I see it's Dr Winsall. The cave turns into this giant fish head and swallows everything into its big black toothy mouth and everything goes dark. And then I wake up.

Bang and Blast

My lobster alarm clock is beeping its pincers off. Normally it doesn't go off. Normally I wake myself up.

Usually I shut my eyes before I go to sleep and tell my head what time I want. It's pretty effective. I don't know how it works. Once I googled 'head sleep programming' and got 14,600,000 results in 0.3 seconds. They said things like 'Free Science and Engineering software downloads', 'Sleep to succeed' and 'Sleep and dream your way to brilliant ideas', so I still don't know. Sometimes there just isn't an answer, even in 14,600,000 suggestions. I think that nature is magic and mystical and best left to get on with it (this gets 6,270,000 results). Bodies and brains are amazing.

I put a cross on my brain-versus-alarm-clock chart.

It's only the second cross in the alarm clock column. The first one was after me and Dad had stayed up late watching *The NeverEnding Story*, which Dad had said would be brilliant. We also ate a giant slab of Dairy Milk Mint Crisp and half a bag of marshmallows. My stomach did a lot of gurgling and I had dreams about flying dragons. People with swords kept charging at me and trying to chop my arms and legs off. I don't think this was a fair brain-versus-alarm competition. It'd be like taking the alarm's battery out and dropping it into a glass of Irn-Bru and then putting it back in again to see what happens. It might completely break the clock. Not that I'm saying my brain's broken. It's just that its usually top turn at doing what I ask it, when I really need it.

I go downstairs. Dad's in the kitchen. 'Ay up, chuck,' he says and does the funky chicken. He holds his coffee mug up. 'Strong stuff, keep well clear.' He's already wearing his work T-shirt. 'Bang and Blast' it says on the front in blue. On the back it says 'Done and Dusted' and there's a picture of a pile of rubble getting swept up with a broom with a smiley face. Dad drinks the last bit out of his mug. 'Gotta go to . . .'

'Bang!' I shoot him down with a finger gun before he finishes. He staggers into the fridge.

'Blast,' he says and detonates me. I explode on the carpet. We lie there dead on the floor for a minute. 'Early shift,' he says and gets up.

'Again?'

'Non-adhesive vinyl tiles await.' He pours me a bowl of Hoops, gets the milk out the fridge. Dad's shop is called Bang and Blast. It's not actually Dad's but it is where he works. The owner is Howard. He smells of chickens and only comes in on Wednesdays. Howard is like one of those elasti-men you get in party bags. His arms pop out the ends of his checked shirts. He has hair like open curtains, a moustache the colour of Crunchie wrappers and many toothpicks. He's the only person in Stepson with cowboy boots.

'All righty.' Dad points his fingers up to the ceiling and shoots. This is what Howard does too. He also says 'sure thing, partner' and 'howdy'. Dad dances two Hoops out of my bowl and on to the worktop. 'Aargh, don't eat us,' he says. I lick them off and crunch them down. 'You okay for school stuff?' He opens my rucksack, and looks in. I nod and zip it back up. 'Good lad,' he says and ruffles my hair. The kitchen clock sings the call of the barn owl. It has different birds for different hours: the nightingale is ten o'clock, the great spotted woodpecker four. The barn owl means six. Dad sticks a banana in his pocket and heads for the door.

I think of the dream, of Dr Winsall. 'What did he say?'

'Who?'

'You know who.'

'Dr who?'

'Yeah, him.'

'He said he wanted to save the universe.' He winks at me. 'Take it easy, buddy,' he says and waves. Then he's off, out the door, into the street, off into the world.

I finish the Hoops, have a glass of no-bits orange and take a tin of beans out of the cupboard.

Beans?

Yeah beans.

Beantastic

Beans are a signal. A tin of beans left out means I'm off swimming. You might think that tuna would be a better choice, cos it has a picture of fish on it. But it's on a higher shelf than the beans and sometimes we don't have any. But there's always beans, loads of beans. Beans are a cert. Me and Dad get them from Aldi. I say, 'Do we need more beans, Dad?' and he says, 'I's bean wondering if you were going to ask,' and I say 'four tins?' and he says 'beantastic,' and I say 'bean anywhere good lately,' and we make up as many bean jokes as we can think of. Sometimes I say, 'How about the ones with sausages?' and he says, 'You could get two tins for the price of those.' So I say, 'Shall I get two more then?' and he says 'righto, beanio.'

After, in the car, we have a Twix each, cept they're called Jive bars. I make mine into fangs. Sometimes Dad makes his into eyebrows, but not on hot days.

I think about this when I get the tin out and it makes me smile. This is another reason why I choose beans for my signal. Tuna just makes me think of dolphins getting stuck in nets.

So . . .

Dive

I stick my trunks on, the ones with the floating slugs on surfboards. Which I like as they are an anomaly. I have different suits for different seasons. Right now it's that autumn in between. And sunny. So I go with the trunks.

Kids round here roam. Everyone does it. We have territories like African wild dogs. Sometimes people fight it out. Mainly we just know it. Jamie Watts rules on land. My space is the sea.

I swim before school. Every day. Early.

Mum says I was born in a blow-up birth pool and I haven't stopped kicking since. I cried when they took me out the water. Stopped when they put me back in. I was a water baby, a bath baby, a slithery pink thing.

The sea is in my blood.

I wrap myself up in the penguin towel, I don't put any clothes on, no shoes either. No one can nick them if I haven't got any. I grab a bag of Scampi Fries, put my goggles round my neck and leg it down to the beach. When I get to the sand I roll the fries inside the towel, chuck it behind a rock and keep running into the sea till it's deep enough to dive. Then I do. I let the water go over all of me, like its swallowing me up. The cold stings my brain. I stretch my arms out and kick and Jamie Watts and the dream and Dr Winsall and everything flow out of my head and into the water like ink leaking out, like a little black cloud floating away.

Until I open my eyes.

What?

The *THING* is there.

It's very real and unimagined.

It's a mackerel. Staring right at me, its face is so close its lips knock into the front of my panoramic lens. I don't know if it's the same one as last time. I don't know how you tell. It's like people with tortoises who say one is called Colin and the other is Theresa and they both look exactly the same. Do they really know or are they just guessing?

I look left and right. Up and down. Seabed and shadows and rock and blue. The rest of the shoal is nowhere to be seen. I look straight out.

The eyes are still there.

Staring.

Mackerel swim at 5.5 metres per second. They are the prey of tuna, whales, dolphins, sea lions, sharks, turtles and pelicans.

They're scared of everything.

This one should be scared of me.

It isn't.

We flow in and out. Together. Like there's magnets stuck in our brains.

Up on the surface it starts to rain. Just a bit.

The fish looks twitchy.

Maybe he doesn't like rain.

Maybe he's bored.

He cocks his head like he wants something. I don't know what.

We float.

We bob.

We stare.

I need air. I surface, breath and dive. Is he gone? Nope.

The water blocks my ears. My head buzzes and tinks. It's a strange kind of no sound. Like me and the mackerel are stuck in a lift together.

I wonder if it'll let me touch it.

I bring my hand up.

He looks at me like I'm crazy. Hurt. Like a cat that

you've just offered a fruit pastel to.

Okay.

He doesn't want to be my pet then. Not a petting pet anyway.

I pull my hand back.

I look at his scales. There's a scar on his side, like a tree trunk that's grown round barbed wire. I wonder if he got stuck on a plastic can holder? I'm embarrassed about our wastefulness.

He stares at me.

I stare.

He stares.

The water pushes us about.

He opens his mouth. The inside is smooth and pearly white.

FishBoy,

he says, and my heart stops.

Kezdodik

He moves his fins as if trying to get me to talk, to coax some words out of my mouth. His eyes are bright and bouncy. His voice is deep like tunnels. I don't know what to say. What does he want me to say?

Kezdodik

Kezdodik

'**WHAT?**' I say.

The fish cocks his head like I'm a total idiot for having no idea what *kezdodik* means and swims off. I get the feeling that if fish had doors, it'd be slamming one in my face right now.

Run

I get out, grab the towel and run.

I boy run through the rain, I fish dodge the hawthorn hedge with thorns like razors, I fish boy jump over the 'Look Out For Frogs' sign and into the kitchen. I look at my watch. Seven minutes eleven seconds. First best-without-shoes time.

Mum is up, in her nightie. In the garden. She's sitting on the green and white striped swing chair reading *Take a Break*.

I stand by the chair, dripping. My chest goes up and down fast. I try to make it stop, to make it normal again.

'Hi,' I say.

'You okay?' she says.

'Fine,' I say. 'Great.' My heartbeat makes my head say *Kezdodik, Kezdodik, Kezdodik*. I wonder if I'm going crazy.

'Do you believe in . . .' I fiddle with the hem of the towel, 'stuff.'

'What stuff?'

'I don't know,' I say and look away.

'God, ghosts, the marshmallow man? What?' She makes her hand into pincers and grabs my leg.

'It doesn't matter.' I pull away and wrap myself up in the towel and sit next to her on the swing. We rock together. I look at the photo in the magazine, of Angelina Jolie in a swimsuit stroking her hair back, coming out of the sea. It makes me think of when we used to do that, when Mum taught me to swim.

'Dr Winsall is doing some tests,' she says.

'Why?'

'You know why.' She strokes my arm.

I don't actually. All I know is that last June Mum got chickenpox. She had a fever so high she didn't know who any of us were. And then she got better. Except she didn't. Not really. A ball of water drips down my forehead off my fringe and runs down my leg. I wonder if it's a drop the fish has touched. 'I don't like microscopes,' I say. 'People should stop poking things about. People should just let stuff be. Let it live.'

'What if the thing's not working,' she says. 'What if it's gone wrong?'

I look at the drip soaking into the concrete. 'Nature'll sort it out. Nature's the best. Nature can fix things if we just leave it to it. It always does. It always finds a way.'

The sun shines in Mum's hair making it go all different colours. Her best friend Leslie dyes it every month. So far they've got through every dye except Starry Night Blue Black on the Personal Hygiene shelf of John's Corner (which is actually in the middle of the street) Shop. Right now it's Chestnut Brownie, with bits of Honeysuckle that never quite washed out.

'It's like king fish,' I say still staring. 'It's like flashes.'

'Where?' Her eyebrows go bendy.

'Your hair looks kind of stripy.'

'Tell me about it,' she says and shuts her eyes.

'The king fish or the hair?'

'The fish,' she says and bats me on the leg.

'They're massive,' I say. She nods, so I know she's listening even though her eyes are closed. I switch my brain over to my David Attenborough *Africa* DVD box set. 'They're as big as a man and really good hunters, really savage. But there's this one time every year when they stop doing what they're doing. All over the ocean they all stop and they stop being themselves and being by themselves and they all get together. Which is really unusual. They swim into fresh water out of the sea and when they go they all calm down. They stop being savage and they stop hunting. They just swim round and round and round in a big circle, this massive circle of fish. And they don't go there to breed, or hunt or feed. They just swim round all chilled out and it looks beautiful, like a painting. Then they go back down the river. No one's told them to stop and no one knows why. They don't need to know why, do they. Cos it's what they do, what they need to do. It's just how they are. They don't need poking about to find out. They need to be left alone to get on with it.'

Mum strokes my arms. I see that my hands have clenched up into balls. As she strokes them they ease out again and my shoulders go down. I look at how her breath is making the Scottie dogs move on her nightie. They're jumping up and down, but really slowly. I think about us in the park jumping on the red elephant and bouncy fire engines when I was little. When we went on the tyre swing, the way she'd fall over pretending like she was dead when the tyre touched her. Dad used to chase us and we'd run down the lane and over the field and I thought it would always be like that. We'd run like we could do it forever, like we'd never stop and our legs would just keep on going, on and on and on.

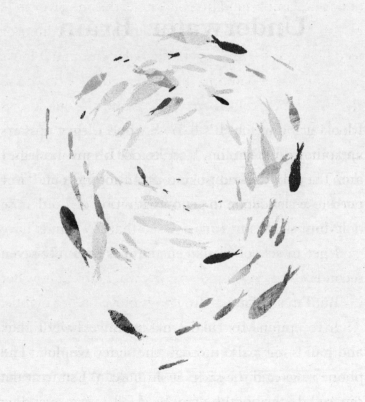

Underwater Brain

I look at my watch. It's 8.37. School! I leg it upstairs and put my uniform on. It sticks a bit on my wet legs. I slam the door and run. I go round lampposts and over curbs like a shoal on the run from a pod of bottlenose dolphins.

I get to school in sixteen minutes and fifty-seven seconds.

But I'm still late.

In reception Mrs Tulan looks at my wet hair dribble, and hands me a slip through the slidey window. The phone rings and she slides it shut again. I stare at the slip and think about the mackerel.

I walk into class thinking about that fish. My feet go

Kezdodik

Kezdodik

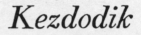

Kezdodik

Sir David says, 'There are many extraordinary creatures not in the limelight.'

Mrs Ahira says, 'Billy.'

I say, 'What?'

She says, 'Focus.'

I spend the day like a fish zombie and walk home with an underwater brain.

I go up the steps and into the kitchen.

Dad is hydrating noodles with the light-up kettle.

'Hi,' I say.

'Howdy.' He sprinkles the yellow powder into the bowls. It spins. My head spins. The room spins. He looks me in the eye, 'You okay?'

'Hmmn,' I shrug.

'Hmmn?' he says.

'Hmmn,' I say

'Just hmm?' he says.

'Hmmn.' I watch a bluebottle hide in the basil plant.

'Okay.' He picks up both bowls. 'Let's eat before we break into a musical.'

Giant Kelp

Next morning I don't swim. Not today.

I keep checking my skin to see if it is coping without the salt dunk. It is.

My brain isn't though. It's full of talking mackerel.

I don't tell anyone.

I get a lot of teacher eyebrow attention and three *what's up with you* elbow pokes from Patrick, plus a cheek flicking when I miss the end of his 'rub-a-dub' card trick. The flicking only stops when I promise to go round to his after school and *act like a normal person*.

Mum lets me go, as long as I promise to eat three carrot sticks on the way.

I wonder what to tell Patrick. Everything? Nothing?

I walk down the steps thinking.

Fish

   Boy

Fish

   Boy

Fish

And along our street.

It's long with houses on both sides packed in but pretty. We've always lived here. It feels good. Like the shape of a happy thing. Like when you get up off a bean bag and leave a dint. It's cosy. You can tell you've been there. The dint says you've had a nice comfy time.

I stop at the crossing. If you look straight on you can see the sea from here. You can also see Zadie's house. Hers is sea view, beach front. We're not. You can see the beach from my room though. From all the bedrooms. You just have to climb a bit, that's all.

I look down the road, to John's Corner Shop, the street that leads up to school, into town. I see Zadie coming out in a zombie T-shirt with a Bounty. She stops and stares. I panic and wave. I hope that she's too far away to see the colour of my face.

She waves back.

Sir David says, 'Given the right environment giant kelp can grow between seven and twelve centimetres every day.'

I cross over on to Crawcrook Drive feeling very tall, like I have grown seven centimetres in the last minute and I think, *everything, I'll tell Patrick everything.*

Free

I go past Welford Street. Down Muston Road.

The houses thin out. The gardens get bigger. The cars get shinier.

I see the sign for Heather Hill Close. 'Building communities,' it says in a speech bubble from a hedgehog.

Patrick's is number 21. It's on its own, detached, not in row like ours. I look around. No one's playing in the gardens. No one's playing in the street either. A tabby cat looks at me and runs away under a bush. I look for Sir David but he's paddling downstream in a dugout. 'Perhaps the musk rats are paying rent by providing fresh bedding for the lodge,' he says. I raise an eyebrow, but he's off, downriver and says no more.

Nature is distracting. I turn back to the door and ring the bell.

When I get in I have to take my shoes off. The house smells of paint and new carpets.

Patrick's mum slices up an apple and gives us half each in two plastic bowls. I take the blue one. We eat them in the food zone, on chairs with plastic wrapped cushions. My fingers make dirty marks on the apple slices. Patrick's sister comes in wearing a Little Miss Messy T-shirt, shouts, 'Nah ni, Nah ni, Nah ni,' and bangs a toy vacuum cleaner against the door frame really hard. BHAM, BHAM, BHAM. It leaves blue plastic marks. She has to sit in the naughty zone and screams her head off. As we go upstairs Patrick pulls a plastic horse from out of his nose and hands it to her. She stops crying and grabs his legs like a northern clingfish (which can actually hold up to 230 times its own bodyweight and inspired the production of superglue). His mum sprays and wipes where we have been.

In Patrick's room there's boxes on shelves with labels: SPACE, CARS, WAR, LEGO. I pick up the Millennium Falcon out of the LEGO one. I try and adjust the laser cannon. It won't budge.

'My mum makes me stick it together with superglue,' he says.

'Why?'

'So the bits don't go missing.' He whacks it on the windowsill: no bits fall off. We take out the 'SPACE' box and look out of the window with telescopes for interesting things.

'Over there!' he says.

I see the tabby cat squatting down in the garden, lifting its tail. 'Is that yours?' I say.

'Buzzard!' he says. 'In the tree.' I don't see anything.

We look at each other's eyeballs through the scopes and watch his *Masters of Magic* DVD. A woman in a gold bikini goes into a cupboard and gets divided up into three parts. The magician slides her stomach backwards and forwards, away from her body. The woman wiggles it to prove she's still alive. Watching the wiggling makes me feel strange.

Patrick switches off the TV and turns round. 'Ta-da,' he says and makes a tortoise appear out of his trousers.

'Oh,' I say and pull a face by accident. I wonder how long the tortoise has been sitting there.

'This is Rango,' he says, putting him down on the bed. He doesn't look too fazed by the trouser experience. I stroke the scales on his legs. He doesn't seem to like this cos he moves them away. I watch him breathing, his neck going in and out under his chin. He yawns his snappy little mouth. The tiny pink tongue looks like a beak, like a baby bird.

I look down into the garden. The grass, cut all neat. No flowers, no plants, nothing, not even daisies. 'We should set him free,' I say. 'Just for a bit. We should let him go where he wants.' Patrick lets me carry Rango downstairs, I keep my hand away from his tail in case he gets scared and wees down my sleeve. I put him down on the grass. 'Off you go,' I say and clap my hands as if he's a dog.

'Liberation, liberation!' Patrick shouts. Rango sticks his head back in. When it comes out again we watch him go. He's very fast for a tortoise. I think what the world must look like to him, tiny bumps like mountains, a grass jungle. I wonder if he thinks about it at all or if he just feels like he is swimming, swimming in a giant sea of green.

Rango gets stuck behind a Hawaiian sunrise flowerpot. We get him out with the handy grabber and put him back in his run. Patrick's mum comes out with a plastic bag over her hand and picks up the cat poo. 'You boys hungry?' she says and slings it in the bin.

'No thanks,' I say, staring at her bag hand. She rubs it with antibacterial cleaner.

51

'I've got something to show you.' Patrick jumps up.

'Like what?' I hope he hasn't got something else down his trousers. 'I don't like tarantulas,' I blurt out.

He squints at me. 'Why would I have a tarantula?'

'Just checking.' Tarantulas like to make their homes in natural crevices.

'Come on,' he says and we go into the garage, through a side door. A corner has been cleared out, a small square of emptiness in amongst a forest of cardboard boxes. We squeeze past two sets of steel shelves into the space. 'It's sort of my magic set-up,' he says. 'Take a seat.' He points to a red stacking chair. I sit down.

'What're they for?' I point to a massive pile of playing card packs.

'Don't touch those!' He spins round.

'I'm not!' I pull my finger off the deck.

'I have different packs for different days,' he says and picks up a black plastic tray from on top of a multipack of WD40 cans. He swooshes the black cloth off the top. In the middle of the tray there's a kind of mini guillotine with a hole in. There's also a carrot. He puts the carrot through the hole and slices it in half. I don't say anything but I notice how he's clearly had this set-up waiting, on the tray. It's a nice feeling.

52

'Put your finger in,' he says.

This is not a nice feeling. 'Right now?' I happen to like my fingers. 'Can't you just use another carrot?'

'Billy.'

'What?' My hands are tucked under my armpits.

'Don't you trust me?'

Are you kidding? I think but don't say. 'Yeah.' I shrug, my voice coming out a little squeaky. My hands stay put.

'Pick a number between six and ten.' He puts the tray down on the lawn mower.

'That's a small range. Shouldn't it be—'

'Just pick one.'

I think hard. Last time I picked three, so if we're going for the same number formation I guess he's guessing I'll pick seven. 'Eight,' I say.

'Look under the No More Nails.'

I turn to the metal shelves and lift up the tube. There's a yellow post-it underneath. *I knew you would pick eight*, it says.

'Hmmn.'

'Finger,' he says and points at the guillotine.

I wonder which one I would mind missing most. I choose my left little finger, nearly put it in and pull back. 'Have you done this before?'

'What do you think?' He puts his hand to the top of the slicer part.

'How would I know?'

'Trust me. Okay?' He stares right at me. I stare right back. I think of Jamie Watts, of the yard, of the rescue.

'Okay,' I say and put it in and shut my eyes. My shoulders go up.

'Ready?' I wonder how much blood will squirt out, if you can sew a finger back on. He lifts the blade. 'Three, two, one . . .'

Air whooshes past my skin. '*Kezdodik*,' I say. It just sort of pops out before I can stop myself. The blade clicks down.

'Kezdodik?' Patrick says. I open my eyes. The room goes fuzzy. My finger is still there. I pull it back. 'Kezdodik?' he says, like he knows something I don't.

'It was a fish!' I can't believe the words are coming out of my mouth. Sirens start going off in my head. SHUT UP SHUT UP SHUT UP ones. But I don't shut up. My hands are sweating. 'A talking fish,' I say. 'It was a mackerel.' I feel the need to be specific, like explaining everything makes more sense. 'With a scar and a kind of weird look like . . .' I try to do the look. 'It knew my name.'

Telling him feels as if a bubble that's been stuck in my chest weighing me down is floating away, like I'm light, free, like anything is possible . . .

Then it doesn't.

Idiot

I slam back down to earth. As if I fall so hard I make a giant hole in the ground. Like a Hummer dropped from a helicopter. Like Wylie Coyote over the edge of the canyon. Like there's a me-shaped hole in the garage floor. Because I realise that I've just said the most stupid thing possible to my only actual friend, that I look like a complete and total idiot and I wish I could just disappear.

On the other side of the garage door I hear a horn play the 'Dukes of Hazard' tune. It's a total miracle. It's Dad. I get up so fast the red chair clatters on the floor. It knocks the tray. The tray wobbles, then falls. The guillotine falls too and cracks on the floor.

I look up at Patrick. I don't know what to say. So I

don't say anything. I just run. I run through the garage, out the door, through the garden and into the street, without looking back. Dad is waiting with Howard in his red Cadillac with bullhorns. I get in. Patrick's mum frowns from the window. Howard draws his fringe curtain back out of his eyes, flicks a toothpick between his teeth and presses the horn again. He starts the engine and the CD player plays Hank Williams singing 'Hey Good Lookin''. Howard likes his music loud. The windows are down. This makes the music blast out down the street. Faces appear in the windows of the other houses. Most of them are frowning.

Howard blows smoke off his pistol fingers and waves. I wonder if he's ever been embarrassed in his life.

'You okay?' Dad says, clocking the colour of my face.

'What happened to the van?' I say.

'Van's bust,' Dad says. We are shouting with our hands cupped over our mouths to be heard above Hank.

'Yes, siree,' says Howard and makes the pistol hand point up to the roof of the car. I am squeezed in the back in between piles of Dixieland chicken takeaway boxes and Budweiser six packs. I'm glad the windows are down or it would stink.

'Fancy the scenic route, guys?' says Howard.

'Not really,' shouts Dad.

'No,' I say. I just want to go home, right now. I wish the Cadillac could teleport.

I don't know if Howard hears us or not but he says 'Righty-ho, partners' and turns off for a detour by the sea, down Marine View, Jamie Watts territory. Great. I wonder how low I can go in the chair. I slide till my knees buckle on the seat in front. Not low enough. I take a Dixieland box and hold it up to the window by my face. My legs stick to seat leather.

In my head I ask Sir David but even he just holds up his hands and shrugs. 'Coral polyps extrude their guts and eat their rivals alive,' he says. Great.

Then I see Jamie. And Archie. And Oscar. They point and laugh. Howard just waves and smiles. He blows the horn. I push the box up higher. As we go past, Jamie is shouting, 'Nice wheels, man.' Archie is making the loser sign. Oscar has a rock in his hand. He throws it but it misses and hits a parked BMW X3 on the other side. The BMW's alarm goes off and they run.

'Hey, aren't those your Nikes?' Dad says.

I don't say anything. I just keep seeing Patrick's face. I am such an idiot. The words swim round and round in my head like a goldfish going past a sunken pirate ship skeleton wreck. *Idiot. Idiot. Idiot.*

Seventy Per Cent
of the Earth

I don't notice the rest of the journey home. My brain
has gone on freeze-frame. Like it's taken a picture of
Patrick for a screen saver. I don't even notice that we
have stopped and that Dad has opened the door.

'Getting out, son?' he says.

'That's the Caddy effect,' says Howard. 'Once
you're in, you don't ever want to leave.' He strokes the
dashboard like he's touching someone's face.

'Cheers, Howard,' says Dad.

'No problemo,' says Howard. I peel myself off the
leather and feel the red lines on the backs of my legs.

'Say thanks to Howard,' says Dad.

'Thanks to Howard,' I say and click the door shut.

Howard restarts the engine and the CD shuffles and plays 'Stand By Your Man'. When we get inside Dad makes some beans. There isn't anything else and we can't go shopping without the van. Mum is asleep upstairs. Again.

We eat on knee trays by the TV and watch championship darts. Dad taps his fingers and doesn't jump up, or punch his fist at the one hundred and eighties. Neither do I. I don't eat many beans either. Neither does Dad. Phil 'The Power' Taylor loses the match and we switch off.

I put my tray down and see there are letters on the table. 'Has you *bean* going to open these?' I say. Dad just shrugs and goes into the kitchen.

'Bills,' he says. 'It'll just be bills.'

'This one isn't.' I pull the top one out. It's from Mum's job. I know as it says 'Ferry Good Travel' on the envelope in blue with a picture of a ferry in sunglasses waving two palm trees in one hand and a cocktail in the other.

He takes the letter and rolls his eyes. 'Great stuff,' he says. He doesn't open it. Mum hasn't been at work for a while now. I don't know how long. I gave up crossing the days off on my Moods of Nature calendar.

I lie on the carpet and try to build a tower with the

Flamenco drink mats. It keeps falling over. I give up.

*

When I go to bed I look up at my Oceans of the World poster. Sir David says, 'Over seventy per cent of the earth is covered by sea. The Pacific Ocean alone covers half the globe. You can fly across it nonstop for twelve hours and still see nothing more than a speck of land.' Our planet is a blue planet. I am just a tiny speck bobbing on the surface. From space you can't even see Stepson beach at all cos in amongst everything else it's so small. This makes me feel strange but not any better. I think of global warming and ice caps melting and water rising and rising and covering everything, till there's no land left and no school and no things to break down and go wrong and I think this might help me get to sleep, but it doesn't.

Coming or What?

I do fall asleep though.

    I know cos I have this dream.

    It is dark. Watery dark and floaty.

    I am in the sea.

    The mackerel is here.

    It swims up to my face. Its eyes are big and shiny.

Coming or what?

It says.

Coming or what?
Coming

Or
What?

I wake up with a bump.

Eating Dirt

The next morning I don't swim. I feel sick. I don't even want to go outside.

Patrick must think I'm nuts.

Coming

Or

What?

What.

Definitely what.

I feel dried out and stiff. Like a salt cod on a Norwegian house rack.

It's been forty-eight hours and counting.

I go downstairs. Dad has already got up and gone early, even earlier than the barn owl. He's left his coffee mug out, his favourite one. One side has a picture of a puffin, on the other it says 'Nuffin'. I bought it for him last Christmas. There's something else too – a piece of toast with a smiley face cut out. Dad is great at art. He did a degree in sculpture. On the wall next to the stairs there's these insects he's made, out of wire. The preying mantis is the best. In my bedroom I've got a polar bear made out of Mod Roc hanging over the edge of the wardrobe. In the corner there's a globe we did with a balloon and paper maché. The North Pole is covered in dust. We haven't made stuff for ages. Now he's always so tired. His fingers twitch. I think they're bored behind the desk of Bang and Blast. They need to move, make stuff, be free.

Sir David is watching a family of ring-tailed lemurs eat dirt. 'Soil is thought to help with digestion,' he says, 'but it also provides minerals and even helps with gut parasites.'

Mum comes downstairs. 'You not *bean* swimming,'

She points at the counter, no bean tin.

'I'm ill,' I say. She puts a hand to my forehead. I pull my best sick face.

'Dad out?' she says.

'Uh huh.' I'm trying to sound weak. I see the Ferry Good travel agent's letter open on the table. I look at the ferry logo waving and read the words: 'We are regrettably writing to inform you . . .'

Mum picks up the letter. 'There he is,' she says and looks out the window.

'Who?'

'The bullfinch.' She points into the garden. I pull myself up on to the worktop to see out. I love bullfinches. They're crazies. The way they bounce sideways on the long grasses. We watch it eat a dandelion. It tries to stuff the whole thing into its beak a piece at a time. Peck, peck, peck. The more it stuffs the more bits fall out. It looks around in between each peck like there might be something coming for it, like it needs to watch out. I think of a giant Jamie Watts bird. A Jamie sparrow hawk. And me with no protection. No saviour Patrick bird. The bullfinch flies off.

'I don't think I should go to school today,' I say. Mum looks into my eyes. I look at the floor. My legs hang down on the cupboards. 'Don't make me go.' I lean into her. 'I think I'm going to be sick.' My voice comes out like I'm going to cry.

'Okay,' she says and sighs. She folds the letter up and puts it into her dressing gown pocket. 'Just for today.'

The Sea of Questions

Mum says we're not going to watch TV, we're going to exercise our brains. 'If the body gets sick, you've got to keep the brain alive,' she says. We play Scrabble and Star Wars Labyrinth. You have to keep moving the board around each turn, creating new passageways to get to where you need to be. Mum keeps picking up the character cards and going:

'I've got to find the wrinkly guy.'

'Yoda.'

'The hairy guy.'

'Chewbacca.'

'The need-to-see-the-dentist guy.'

'Darth Maul.'

I win the Labyrinth. Mum wins Scrabble with *existence* on a double word space. In between games Mum rests and I watch my *Frozen Planet* DVD, which is allowed as it's educational. Sir David's voice comes out of the speaker. The wind blows snow over the icy wasteland. 'The frozen seas are worlds unto themselves,' he says. 'Beneath their ceiling of ice they have an eerie almost magical stillness, cut off from the storms that rage above them.' I put my head on Mum's shoulder, on to her fleecy blanket.

It ends and we play Trivial Pursuit. Neither of us is any good. We get a bit daft and laugh at strange things and over a question about the lifecycle of frogs.

'Which country invaded Cyprus in 1974?'

'Haven't got the foggiest,' she says. 'Which Royal invented the dipping headlight?'

I shrug and bulge my eyes. She chucks the card in the air. 'What's the height of a basketball hoop?' Chuck.

'What is a group of bears called?' Chuck.

'A sleuth,' I say.

'Smart arse,' she says but looks kind of proud.

'What do two dings on the Lutine bell signify?' Chuck. Chuck. Chuck.

'It's all so trivial,' she says and laughs. She gets

some out of the box and throws them at me. I throw them back. And then we're both throwing them at each other. They go up in the air and on the floor and behind the sofa. Everywhere. As if it's raining facts, rectangular raindrops. Until the box is empty. We lie on the carpet and move our arms and legs in the sea of questions as if we're swimming, the way you make snow angels. Then we stop. She holds her hand out and I take it. We look up at the ceiling, the big white wavy patterns. It makes my mind go all floaty.

'When are you gonna get better?' I say.

'I don't know,' she says. 'No one knows.'

'Why not?'

'Life is mysterious,' she says. 'There's no sun without shadow, and it is essential to know the night.'

'What?'

'Camus, Albert Camus.' She balances a card on her nose. 'He's a philosopher.'

'Mice can fit through a hole the size of a ballpoint pen,' I say.

'Really?' She rolls her finger, to make a pen size.

'Mum.'

'Yeah.' She squints through the hole. I think about her disappearing down into it. About her disappearing altogether. I try to push the thoughts away. 'I miss swimming with you.'

'Me too, love,' she says and squeezes my hand a bit too tight, 'me too.' We hear the kitchen clock tick. It hits one and makes the call of the chaffinch. 'I need a rest now.' Her eyes look tired. 'You can watch TV if you want.' I help her up. She gives me a hug. 'Can you put the cards away?' she says. I pull a face. 'And Billy . . .'

'What?'

'Back to school tomorrow,' she says and my heart dive-bombs. She goes upstairs. I make my hand into a mechanical grabber. Up, out, over, release. Sometimes the cards go in the box, mostly they don't. I watch it filling up as if it's counting the time down to tomorrow, as if each card's a minute. I move slow cos I don't want the box to be full. I want to pull them all out again, so tomorrow never comes and I can stay here in the in-between time, where it's safe, forever.

Unexplained Mysteries of the Universe

U.S. Navy Avengers Flight 19

On December 5th, 1945, Flight 19 set out in a Gruman TBF Avenger (see fig.5). There were five highly experienced pilots. It was a routine patrol. The weather was fine and sunny.

They left at 1.15 p.m.

At 3 p.m. flight leader Lieutenant Charles C. Taylor contacted the operations tower in distress. They were lost. None of the compasses were working. Everything looked wrong.

They were never seen again.

The Navy investigated but found nothing to explain the disappearance. There were many searches, but no one has ever found Flight 19.

I think about Mum.

I think about her disappearing.

I shut the laptop.

Kesz

The next morning I pick up my bag, ready for the longest day of my life. No more Patrick. It's over. Who wants to be friends with a weirdo? Jamie Watts will eat me alive.

Sir David says, 'For baboons, it's not how big they are, but who they know, that counts.'

Dad has left a picture of a doughnut singing, 'I believe I can fly.' I draw a coffee mug around the doughnut, its head dunked under the coffee and a giant mouth heading its way. To toothy doom. Then I feel bad and scribble it out and turn the scribble into a big cloud. A black one.

Idiot, idiot, idiot. My head chants. I wonder who Patrick was hanging out with yesterday, who he'll be hanging out with now instead of me. We didn't even make it past the first week.

I walk down the street, looking at the cracks in the pavement and stepping over them, looking at my squashed-up feet in the gym shoes. If I keep looking down I won't be able to see everyone laughing at me. It must have spread round the school pretty fast. Fish Boy talks to fish. It's stupid enough to be interesting. Interesting enough to get passed on and on and on. I wonder who Patrick told first.

I see Zadie Eccleston's silver Doc Marten laces. 'Hi,' she says and walks next to me. Her hair bounces. I don't say anything. She must have heard by now. She must think I'm crazy.

Sir David says, 'Vampire bats scratch each others backs and share their meals of blood.' Zadie just shrugs and walks past. When I look up she's already reached the end of the street. Zadie Eccleston walks at the running speed of a black spiny-tailed iguana.

I get to Boothby Street and wait until I hear the bell and then I go in, head down, not seeing anyone, not looking up at all.

I avoid Patrick. This is made easier by him being in Mr Sim's class rather than mine. He has English, I have French. He has science, I have food tech. I have cross-country running, he has personal social health education. We both have maths but he's in the top set and I'm not. This just leaves lunch and break times to sort. Avoiding everyone else is harder.

At break I hang around behind the DT workshop block. People don't go there because it's dark and because of the bins. I sit on the rusty manhole cover behind the black bin. There's a pile of fresh sawdust next to the green one. The smells come one after the other, like they're playing pile-on, trying to keep on top. Rot, wood, rot, wood, turpentine, rot, wood, rot. The wood smell is actually nice. I notice how noticeable things are when you're not doing anything.

Zadie appears from nowhere, like a musk deer. They're expert hiders. They only let you see them when they want you to.

We stare at each other. Mist rises off the bins.

The bell goes.

She strides off and the skull key ring on her rucksack jingles along behind.

*

Avoiding Patrick goes well until the final bell. I'm walking down the hall, past Year Six's Save the Rainforest posters to the coat racks when he catches up with me.

'Billy.' He taps me on the shoulder. I shrug his hand off and keep walking. It's so embarrassing. I don't even look at him. He speeds up and goes in front of me. He stops. I have to stop too or I'll get his niceday ring binder spine in my peanuts. Not that it's a threat, it's just how he's carrying it.

'What's up with you?' he says.

'Nothing.'

'Where've you been?'

'Nowhere.' I look away. 'What do you want?' He takes a step back. Becky and Sheree walk past, look at each other and laugh. *You told Becky?* I think but don't say.

I go to start walking again. I feel redder than the foam balls.

'Stop!' He puts a hand out on to my chest. '*Kesz*,' he says. Archie and Oscar go past and make kissing noises. Patrick doesn't even notice.

'Get off.'

He looks into my eyes. 'I believe you,' he says. '*Kesz*.' He looks round both ways to check no one is listening. He leans over and says it by my face. '*Kesz kezdodik*, it's the other half of the code.'

78

Cool

Patrick texts his mum and we walk back to my house. We talk about the pet values of guinea pigs versus bearded dragons. He doesn't look at me funny. Things feel okay.

He buys us two ninety-nines from the Mr Whippy van. The sign on the back says MIND THAT CHILD with a cross-eyed Donald Duck eating an ice pop. 'I got monkeys' blood on,' he says. I stare at the sauce dripping off mine.

'Thanks.'

'It's not from real monkeys.'

'Yeah,' I say, 'I know.'

'It is from real beetles though,' he takes a big lick round the side of his. 'Cochineal, crushed beetles.'

I look at mine and shrug. We get to my steps. 'This is it,' I say and sit down. I take the flake out and eat the ice cream off it like a spoon. 'They taste good, beetles.' I look at Patrick. He's a very messy eater. 'Where'd the other colours come from then?'

'Yellow's crushed bees, green's grass snakes, purple's I dunno . . .'

'Squeezed scars.' I make like I'm squashing my head and stick my tongue out the side of my mouth. 'They wring out scarred people's faces.'

'Yeah.'

Francine from up the street goes past on her Cosmic Light scooter. 'All right, Billy,' she says and smiles, looks Patrick over.

'You wanna go inside?' I say. He nods. We break off the bottom of the cones to drink the ice cream out, crunch up the rest and go in.

Round ours we don't do zones like Patrick's house. We do spillage and mess and stuff, lots of stuff. Patrick keeps touching things and saying 'cool' and 'awesome'. We walk through the kitchen and I show him the back garden. I like doing the house tour. I used to do them when we had people over. Which we haven't. For ages.

Our back garden is 'very unexpected'. That's what people always say when they see it for the first time.

There's walls all around and a gate in the back one. You'd never know it was here if you hadn't been. It's like an oasis in between concrete. Mum says that's why they bought the house, why she fell in love with it. 'A gate in a wall proves anything's possible,' she says. 'There's always a way through.'

I show him the strange weed thing that's grown higher than my head by the side wall. 'What's it gonna be?' He boings the stalk so the stem sways into my face.

'How would I know?'

'Strange,' he says. 'What if it grows into an alien plant?'

'What if it does?'

'What if it eats you while you're asleep.' He makes his arm into jaws and bites my head off. We fall over on the grass and roll about. I pull myself up on to my knees and rub my elbow, get the bits out of my hair.

'Wanna go upstairs?' I say.

'Okay.'

On the way up I show him the bathroom and the spare room. He stares at the flying man sculpture over the bath. 'Superman,' he says and stretches a leg out as if he's flying. The spare room's kind of an office. We keep loads of stuff in there. Shelves and shelves of

81

it. *Teach Yourself Russian*, two plastic daffy ducks, Dad's collection of snow globes. I miss out Mum and Dad's room with Mum still in it and we go up the last flight of stairs to mine. Up to the old attic.

'Nice preying mantis.' He stops on the way up to stroke the metal legs.

'They say when they made my room, when they converted the attic they heard this yapping, this howling of a dog like it was trapped in a wall. And when they were done, doing the plastering and painting on the last day, they went in and found these paw prints on the floor.'

I go in first and hide behind the door. When Patrick comes through I jump at him and bark like a dog. He looks properly terrified. I start laughing. I can't stop. He climbs on top of me and raises the fingers of steel. 'Sorry.' I bite my lip. 'I've stopped laughing, promise.' I grab my sides to make myself stop. He puts the hands down and starts to howl. Then we both lie there howling.

I think of Sir David watching timber wolves running over the slopes of Canada. 'Wolves howl to warn neighbouring packs to keep their distance, but they also do so to reunite with their own pack if it's got scattered after a long hunt.' I feel our howls rise up together, out of our chests. It feels good.

It's a bit weird having Patrick in my room. He keeps picking things up.

'Range Rover Mark One.' He pulls the model out of my cube shelves. 'Nice.' He turns it round in his hands and puts it back in a different place.

'Thanks,' I say and move it back, where it's meant to go. 'Airfix kit, over a hundred parts.' I look at the box. The GO ANYWHERE VEHICLE it says.

He takes my electric guitar off the stand. 'Awesome!' He jumps up and down and headbangs.

'Don't!' I take the guitar. 'My mum's asleep.' I put it back on the stand.

'Why?'

'She just is.'

He looks through my board game stuff and pulls out Wings of War. 'Cool, let's play this!'

We don't talk about the fish. It's nice to just do stuff for a bit.

We sweep a pile of clothes under my bed and set it up. I'm the Albatros; he's got the Fokker Triplane – guest's privilege. The Fokker does different moves, has got a tighter turning circle. We play for fifty-seven minutes. He wins – the Fokker usually does. We shake on it and he puts the cards back in the box. I straighten out the bent ones with my sleeve and slide the box back on the shelf. 'Sorry,' I say.

'About what?'

'Today.' I turn round. 'And before. Sorry about your guillotine.' I picture it crashing to the floor when I ran. I picture Patrick's face.

'I fixed it.' He shrugs, 'with the superglue.'

'I thought . . .' I sit down and start fiddling with an Angry Birds sock on the carpet. 'I thought . . .'

'You thought I was a loser,' he says.

'*No!*' I am genuinely surprised at this, the word comes out louder than I mean it to. Why would he even think that? 'I thought you'd told everyone,' I say. 'About IT.'

'Oh.' He looks sad.

I feel bad. I make the sock into a hand puppet and wave it in front of his face saying, '*Kezdodik Kezdodik,*' and bite him with it until he smiles again.

'That sock actually stinks,' he says and laughs.

I make the sock puppet pick up a pair of boxers from under the bed and throw them at him. They land in his face. I laugh. He throws them back and they land in mine. He laughs. I throw a sweatshirt. We're suddenly a little hysterical. There is a blur of throwing things and the room goes fuzzy as my eyes water from laughing. We stop when a pair of jeans with a belt hits me in the nose.

'Oh, sorry!' He puts my eagle sweatshirt down.

'It's okay,' I say and take my hand out of the sock and rub the back of it under my nose. No blood. He's right though – it does stink. '*Kisz kezdodik,*' I say.

'Kesz *kezdodik,*' he says.

'How'd you work that one out anyway?'

'The great Houdini.' He rummages through the clothes, which are now everywhere and opens his bag. He takes out a blank DVD in a see-through case. 'It's Hungarian.' He's stuck a photo on the front. It's of a man tied up in chains. It looks freaky. '*He's* Hungarian.'

I pull a face. 'I wouldn't want to be that guy.'

'It means, ready, begin,' he says and taps the plastic case. 'He used to say it before his act. Before they lowered him into the Chinese Water Torture Cell.'

'The water what?!'

'You've got to say it back to them.'

'The fish?' I realise how crazy this sounds.

'Yeah.'

'Why would fish speak Hungarian?'

'Fish travel.' He shrugs. 'A lot.'

I stare at the picture. Houdini has chains around his hands. His feet. His wrists. His ankles. Everywhere.

If it means ending up like that, if that's what *kesz kezdodik* means, then I'd really rather not. 'I'm not sure, Patrick.' I keep staring at the picture.

'He *gets free*,' he says. 'He's an escapologist, that's the point.'

'I might give the sea a break for a while,' I say.

'Magic is out there,' he says. I laugh but he doesn't. Sometimes laughing happens like that when I'm scared or really upset. It just comes out and sounds all wrong. 'Billy.' He looks totally serious. 'You've got to go back in.'

Mush

At 5.30 Patrick's phone alarm beeps. He has to leave to watch his sister while his mum goes to pilates. We go downstairs.

'Wait a minute,' Mum shouts, just as I'm opening the front door. She comes down too. I stand in front of Patrick so he doesn't notice that she finds this difficult. That this take a while. She's wearing her denim dress and wolf slippers. I am totally thrilled she is actually dressed. 'Hi.' She tucks her hair behind an ear and leans into the door space. 'You must be Patrick.' He reaches out, she ducks but then smiles when he makes a plastic rose appear from her hair.

'Aw, thanks,' she says and offers a hand. 'It's really nice to meet you.'

'Patrick has to hurry,' I say, 'to look after his sister.'
I start closing the door so their hands don't meet. I don't want Patrick to know about Mum. I don't want anyone to know.

'Oh,' Mum says.

'Bye,' Patrick says and nearly falls off the step as I shut the door.

'See you later,' I say through the letter box.

'What was that about?' Mum puts her hand on her hip.

I walk past her into the kitchen. 'Do you fancy meatballs?' Meatballs are my speciality. Actually, it's pretty much the only thing I cook.

'Okay,' she says and follows me with her eyes. 'That'd be lovely.' I go into the kitchen. She puts the Bombay Bicycle Club on the iPod and sits down on the sofa.

I take the meatballs out of the fridge and put them on the fish plate ready for the microwave. I put the kettle on for the pasta. I pour crushed tomatoes out of the jar and into a pan and put the pan on the small ring. I put the pasta in the boiling water and crank the timer round to eight minutes.

After four minutes I realise I forgot to put salt and oil in the pasta water. I put it in and give it a stir. Some of the pieces have stuck to the bottom. I try to unstick them. The timer goes off.

'I'll get that,' Mum shouts. She comes in and carries the pasta pan to the sink to drain. This is the part I don't do. The bit she doesn't let me.

She puts the pasta back in the pan. I tip everything else in too and stir. The spoon goes round. The meatballs break up. Some pasta bits have red on, some don't. The sauce is like a T-shirt that's too small. It doesn't quite fit.

I think about the sand pattern of the puffer fish. It works and works and works to make this amazing spiral. Marking it out with its body. The sea keeps moving the sand all the time and it has to keep going. To keep it in shape. To make it perfect. Sir David says, 'He must work for twenty-four hours a day or the current will destroy his creation.' The camera pulls back and shows the massive spiral he's working on. It's so beautiful.

I look into the pan. It looks like a big pile of mush.

Mum gives me a hug. 'Looks great!' she says.

I get the spiral bowls and spoon it out.

'You okay?' Mum says. She tries to look at me. 'School okay?' I keep spooning. 'Patrick seems really nice,' she says. Her eyebrows look hopeful. The mush does not.

We carry our bowls to the table. I want to say yeah, he might *seem* nice but actually he wants me to talk to a fish that'll probably chain me up at the bottom of the ocean. But I don't. So I just grate a load of cheese on to cover up the mush and say, 'He is. Kind of.'

Hang On

I want to swim. I want it so badly my head feels like it's going to burst. But I'm not going back in the sea on my own. No way.

I lie in bed and poke my ribs to see if it hurts. The bones hurt more than the flesh. I wonder if this is what it feels like to Mum. If she hurts. I wonder if it's like bruises. People only know how much something hurts when the marks show up and by then it's not actually hurting any more. People get what they see. If they see it, they get it. If they can't, you're on your own.

I think of divers in the deep-sea submarine, the walls twelve centimetres thick, of the angler fish where the male bites the female and becomes permanently attached, fed by her bloodstream. I think about how the sea is the most undiscovered place in the world. Sir David says, 'We know more about the surface of the moon, than the abyssal plains.'

I get up and go down to the first floor. The light's on in the spare room. I can hear Dad mumbling about something. I push the door open. He's sitting at the desk looking through papers, a calculator in one hand, a pink highlighter behind his ear. He's got his reading glasses on. He always looks dead different in those, like he becomes someone else.

'Ay up,' he says.

'Ay down,' I say. He smiles.

'You all right, son?' He rubs his head.

'I want to live in a spiral galaxy.'

'Sounds good,' he says and takes the glasses off. 'Can I come?'

'Maybe,' I say and shrug. He holds his arms out and pats his knee. I go and sit on it. He holds me tight. A bit too tight.

'Ow.'

'What?'

'Mind my ribs.'

'Sorry.' He puts his head on the back of my neck and we swing back and forth on the swivelly chair. 'Want to go to Mars?'

'Okay,' I say. We used to play this when I was little. I put my hands over his eyes and shut mine. He holds me on and we pretend we're in a rocket. His legs spin us and we go round and round and round and it feels like we're taking off to Mars. Well, it used to. He stops.

'I feel a bit sick,' I say.

'Me too,' he says. I take my hands off his eyes. He doesn't take his arms off me though. 'Hang on in there, son,' he says. I feel the words against my skin. He holds me tight again and squashes all of me but I don't say anything cos I hardly feel it, I hardly feel it at all.

Milwaukee's 440th Airlift Wing, Plane 680, 1965

In 1965, an experienced crew from the Air Force Reserve Command's 440th Airlift Wing flew from Milwaukee to the Grand Turk Island in the Bahamas.

The plane landed on schedule at Homestead Air Force Base in Florida at 5.04 p.m. They spent two hours and forty-three minutes on the ground.

The plane took off again at 7.47 p.m. and headed south to the Bahamas.

It never reached its destination.

It was a clear night. There was no indication of trouble and all radio communication was routine. When they didn't land, radio traffic controllers called Plane 680. There was no response. There was an expert maintenance crew on board, so if there was a mechanical problem on the flight, there were plenty of people to take care of it.

There was no explanation for the disappearance of Plane 680.

Sometimes stuff just happens. I snap my laptop shut.

Maybe she'll be okay.

Mum.

Maybe the fish is okay.

He seemed nice.

Didn't he?

Did he?

I wonder where the plane went. I wonder what the fish wants. I wonder about weirdness.

Now?

The letter comes on Saturday at breakfast.

'How was the spiral galaxy?' Dad says.

'No chocolate spread.' I put a thick layer on a crumpet. 'So I came back.'

'Understandable,' he says. The toaster pops and the smoke alarm goes off. 'I'm the fire starter!' Dad does his Prodigy impression and whacks the reset button with a broom handle. He sings 'exhale, exhale, exhale', puts the broom back against the wall and passes me a blue envelope. 'This came.'

'That's odd . . .' Mum scrapes butter over the burnt toast. 'No stamp.' She points at the space where it should be. I look at the writing all neat and curled up.

'Gonna open it then?' Dad looks over my shoulder. 'Must be special, no one sends nice letters these days. No one. It's all emails and headaches. Or junk.' He licks peanut butter off his fingers. 'Junk and bills, bills and junk. It's not fair on the trees. What they've had to go through to get to that and then they just get chucked.'

'Or monkeys. The monkeys miss the trees,' I say.

'Yeah they can't swing on an envelope, can they?' He jumps around the kitchen doing a monkey dance.

'And owls,' I say. He flies his arms over the table.

'Buzzards,' Mum says.

'Crows.'

'Wood pigeons.'

'Cuckoos.'

'Jackdaws.'

'They nest in holes actually, not trees,' I say.

'Righto,' Mum shrugs.

Dad does all the birds. Some are better than others. 'You need to work on your buzzard,' I say and he hits me on the head with his Flying Pig tea towel.

'I thought it was all sustainable now anyway,' Mum says. 'They replant them, don't they? They plant what they chop.' Dad looks over at her uneaten toast. She's left half of it. 'Full,' she says and pulls a face. 'I'll give

it to the birds, the poor little treeless birds.' She tears
it into pieces.

'Are you gonna open it or what?' Dad nods at the
envelope.

'Now?'

'Yeah.'

'Right.' I run my fingers over the edges. I don't
know which corner to start from. I tear it open slowly
and look inside.

Believe

I pour the flakes out into my hand.

'Is that it?' says Dad. 'No letter?'

'No,' I say and hide the note that's inside.

'What are they?'

Fish flakes is what they are. 'I don't know,' I say and go red. I put the envelope in my dressing gown pocket.

Mum leans in and looks closer. 'They really stink,' she says and pulls back. 'They could be poisonous.'

'They're not poisonous,' I say. They are sticking to my hand though.

'You should put them down.' Mum prods one with a finger. 'You might get a rash. People send things sometimes, not nice things.' She looks at Dad with concerned eyebrows. He looks back with shrugging ones.

'Yeah, it might be some nutter,' he says.

'Dan!' Mum whacks him.

'I'm just saying . . .' He puts the tea towel over his head and hunches up like he's an old lady. 'Plant the magic seeds, Jack, plant the magic seeds.'

'I wouldn't mind a beanstalk,' Mum says, 'with golden eggs at the top.'

'You'd climb that would yer?' Dad says. 'Tell that to Dr blummin' Winsall.' He shouts up at the ceiling. 'She climbed the bleeding beanstalk, now leave her alone all right!' He gets Mum and lifts her over his shoulder. 'Any golden harps up there?'

'Just three big fat cobwebs.' She taps him on the back. 'Now knock it off.' He puts her down. I try to tip the flakes into the bin. They are totally stuck to my fingers. I try to scrape them off. 'Just going to the bathroom,' I say and go upstairs. I shut the door, put the toilet seat down and take the note out of the envelope.

Dear Fish Boy
    A little something for your friend!

Ha ha.

The *World of Magic* says that the secret to magic is belief. People believe because they want to. I believe in you. I think your fish has something to say. Meet me on the beach tonight at 5.30.

P

I think of how Patrick must have got here to deliver this. I think of him doing his Superman in the air, coming to the rescue, over the houses, one arm out.

I think of the mackerel braving it across the ocean. Alone.

I fold the letter and put it back into my pocket.

I feel bold. I feel brave.

I will be there.

Going Solo

At 5.10 p.m. I take the bean tin out and put it on the worktop. I pull my blue hoody over my head, tuck the exploding volcano towel under my arm and walk to the beach. I am a giant kelp string about to break the surface.

I see Zadie through her feature window, past the coral, in the lounge, watching *MI High*. She turns round. David says, 'Signals from a male wolf spider have to be very carefully delivered because if his female doesn't understand why he's approaching her, she'll eat him.' I duck down and squat along under the rest of the window, hoping she hasn't noticed.

I walk to the steps and look down at the bay.

It's pretty empty. It's always pretty empty. People

usually stick to the cliff paths or walk over to the long sands, the main beach. I like this one. It's always been my favourite. It's always been me and Mum's.

On the right there's boulders with gaps big enough to climb through and hide in and flies and old plastic bags and bottles filled with thunder bugs blown into the cracks. The rocks are big and wonky. I think they're like icebergs. They have things going on underneath in places you can't see.

On the left is the crocodile and bone rocks. People call them that because the ledge looks like a crocodile and the rocks stick out of the sea, like it's chewed someone up and spat out the bones into the water.

And all around everything is the cliff. Like a giant pair of arms. Like it's got its back to the wind so you don't have to take it for a while. When you're in the bay the wind stops.

I look for Sir David. He's hanging up hummingbird feeders in Arizona. 'Meals like these must surely make the difference between life and death,' he says, 'especially for the rufous who still have to tackle the last stage of their two-thousand-mile migration across the bay of Mexico in one single six-hundred-mile flight.' I look at the rufous. They're like eight centimetres long.

I look out at our beach. A sandpiper hops in with a wave, and legs it when it comes back out. A Jack Russell runs to the edge of the cliff, sniffs the air and runs back.

I see Patrick sitting where the wet sand meets the dry, on the dry side. Sitting on the edge.

I run down the steps and leap on him from behind. 'Hey.'

'Hey.' He leans backwards and I fall off. He's stuffing Doritos into his mouth. I stare at the crumbs falling on to the beach. 'Want one?' He offers me the bag. 'They're cheesy.' He rattles them under my nose.

I shake my head and pull back. I don't feel hungry at all. 'Where are your trunks?'

'I'm not coming in.'

'You what?'

'I can't swim,' he says.

'Oh!' I didn't think anyone in our year couldn't swim.

'We never stay in one place long enough.' He looks away. 'And besides, how many people with talking fish do you know?' I shake my head. 'Exactly, Fish Boy. The mackerel has come for you. Just you.'

I turn the words over and over in my head. *The mackerel has come for you.* I wonder if that sentence has been said to anyone else in the world. Ever. 'What's that?' I point to the big white bag next to him.

'Provisions,' he says and takes out a green padlockable notebook and pencil. I look in the bag and see a rope, a chain and a yellow rubber parcel tied with a red belt. He pulls the drawstring on the bag. 'MEGALLAS,' he says, writing the word down in the notebook in capitals and holding it up for me to read. 'It's the code for stop.'

'What's wrong with just stop?'

'Stop isn't Hungarian.'

I want to *Megallas* right now. 'Maybe we should come back tomorrow,' I say and look out at the water. 'It looks like it might get choppy.' The sea is dead calm.

'You can do this, Billy,' Patrick says. 'If you don't you'll spend the rest of your life wondering what might have happened. What you missed. You've just got to go for it.'

Solid

I pull my hoody off and put the towel down on dry sand.

I shine the panoramic goggle lens on my towel and stretch them over my head.

'5.42,' Patrick says, looking down at his watch.

I look down at mine. '5.42.' We're all synced up.

He high-fives me. '*Megallas* is stop,' he says, 'remember that.'

'Okay, okay. I get it.'

He pulls a set of dog tags out from his bag. 'Just in case,' he says.

'Don't they put those on dead people?' I say.

'They're for luck,' he says. 'And they put them on living people *in case* they die.'

I turn the tags over in my hand and see the words MEGALLAS stamped into them.

'Forge Museum,' he says.

I think of the stamping machine there, where you turn the wheel and stamp out one letter at a time. I went in Year Five, for the Materials of Industry project. It must have taken him ages. 'Thanks,' I say and put them over my head. They jangle down on to my chest. Patrick is the best at preparation. They're probably the nicest thing anyone has ever made for me.

Neither of us knows what to say for a minute. We just stand there.

'The navamax triumphs over the janulus,' he says.

I nod at his carnivorous sea slug reference and walk off to the sea. The water looks grey and cold. I let it wash over my feet, then I pull my goggles down over my eyes and run in yelling like Tarzan, 'aaaaa iiiiii aaaa iiii aaaa,' feeling all the fear come spilling out of my mouth.

Ready

I let the water swallow me up, my heart beating. My skin's so glad to be back here. I soak it in and unshrivel.

I shut my eyes for a bit and then open them. Nothing.

No eyes. No fish.

Just nothing.

Bits of bladder wrack weed float by my fingers. Coal dust sparkles over my hands, settles on my skin.

I breathe out and watch the bubbles bubble up to the surface. It might not happen, I think. Not today. Maybe never. Maybe it's given up on me. I float on my back and look up at the sky. Then I feel it on my foot.

I swing over on to my front and look down.

My heart's in my ears.

The mackerel stares at me like a hamster waiting for a mealworm.

'Hi,' I say and try to smile, though smiling in water is tricky.

'*Kezdodik*,' he says, his voice sounds hopeful.

I hold the dog tags in my hand and gather my breath in my chest, ready to push the word out hard.

'*Ketsz*,' I say.

'*Ketsz*,' he says, like he's just been poked with a stick. If fish had eyebrows, I think they would be shocked right now. His eyes bulge. For a minute I think I might have got it wrong. That this is not the right answer. '*Kezdodik*,' he says again and nods, and this is when it starts.

Yes

The mackerel darts under my hand, flicks round and faces front.

He sways his body up, so my hand is resting on his back. It's hard and strong. Bony. A long, slick, muscly bone. I touch him and when I touch him my lungs turn loose. As if I'm sucking air out of the water, as if it's absorbing itself into me. I can breathe. I can stay down here. One touch and I'm not boy any more. He looks up at me. I grin. I am Fish Boy. Now I am Fish.

He moves forwards. I jolt like a Reliant Robin on a tow rope.

We're off.

He starts slowly, takes me through the shallows. He's tight, good at turns. I'm not. We pull up to a rock, shoot off at the last second. My body makes it but my legs are too slow. My ankle hits the rock and bounces off.

'Ow,' I say.

He stops and flicks round. '*Ow?*' He looks confused.

I point at my ankle, at the rock. 'Ow.' He still looks confused. I pretend to bang my head on my hand, in slow motion, through the water. 'Ow,' I say.

He swims up to my face and slaps his tail on it.

It is not slow. It is strong. And fast. '*Ow?*' he says. His voice is deep like tunnels.

'Yes. Ow,' I say and rub my cheek.

'*Ow,*' he says, bouncy happy. Like a kid that's just learned to say *biscuit* and got one. He whacks his head on a rock. '*Ow.*'

'Yes.' I nod. 'Ow.'

He looks dizzy, then snaps back under my hand. '*Ow,*' he says, all proud. I think how fish never touch anything. Except maybe for eating. And that's more sucking and biting than feeling.

We go on, through the sparkly grey.

The salt stings up my nose. I snort it out and feel like laughing. My body is frothing up with bubbles of happy.

We head out into a kind of sea fog. Streaking through. We can see as far as my arms stretch. A space I can reach into. With no edges, just fading into foreverness.

We flick left round the bone rocks, right over barnacle ridges rising up and down. Tough, skin-shredding edges. We go through pillar rocks and flats and steps and blocks. Slabs of grey. Rocks with wrinkles and lines worn in. Creases filled with snails and swaying, spongy green. Then pools, hollows rubbed by the water. Striped pink rock that sparkles.

We go faster. Through a warm current like a blanket, a cold one that makes my goosebumps bump out. Kelp laps my stomach and flaps under my chin. The blue gets higher and wider, like the sea is opening up, like we're swimming into its mouth. I can't believe I'm seeing this stuff. That this is me.

I glance up. The surface is fading away. We go deeper and darker, down and down, towards a light, a tiny silver speck.

The speck gets bigger, brighter. I keep one hand on my fish and one on the dog tags. Tight. It makes me feel as if I'm not doing this alone, like I have an escape route. As we get closer my fish slows down and looks back at me. He cocks his head.

He stops swimming and we drift.

Slowly.

Slowly.

Flash, flash, flash, the light flickers, as if it's trying to tell me something. We get closer and closer. Until we're nose to nose with it and then we stop.

The light is moving. A twisting, turning living thing. I look up and down. I can't look away. There are hundreds of them, thousands, spinning, spiralling. Moving in and out of each other. A mackerel shoal. They go up so high and down so low I can't see either end. Their bodies shiver round and round. The rhythm is hypnotic. It's a DNA double helix. A cathedral lit up in the dark, a spire of silver. A grin bursts up from my stomach to my face. Sir David would love this.

As we get closer I hear them.

A buzzing. Not words. But signals. Thoughts like lights that pass between them. Never bumping, not even touching. Like music. A buzzy head zing. Sweet and high and low and loud, coming together like a hum. Like you can only just pick the voices out if you turn your ears into needles.

I look down at my fish. He looks back at me.

He takes me into the middle of the shoal.

The fish stop.

They turn.

They look.

Thousands of eyes focus on my face, on my black Speedos. Everywhere.

My fish looks left and right, up at me.

'*Fish boy*,' he says.

> *Fish*
>> *Boy*
>
> *Fish*

They stare. They tilt their heads.

Then they all start.

Fish Boy

Fishy boy

Fish

Boy

Fish

They say. Their voices come from all over, high and low and everywhere. They creep closer, heads one way. Heads the other.

A small one shoots out.

Nice?

   Nice?

      Nice?

It says, heading for me. Like I'm something to nibble. Its mouth feels like a vacuum cleaner. It snaps back. Wriggling. Shaking its head.

No nice

   No

No

It looks like it just licked slime. I'm sorry I taste rubbish.

Fish

Boy

Fish

They say.

Fish Boy

The chant's like a wristband at Water World that says *you belong here*. It feels good.

There's a thoughts buzz and they move finger snap fast. The water fills with froth. Bubbles pop over my chest, on the soles of my feet. Their bodies push past. Strong and hard. Past my legs, my face, up and around until everyone's in a line.

My hair flows over my head. I hold on to my fish.

We're a shoal with me in the middle.

There's a pause.

And then we swim.

Go

They say.

Big-shine

Big-shine

Up

We go up. We speed up towards the light, to the surface.

The fish make a wall of silver either side and all around. I'm floating in free space, going with the flow. Through a chink in the bodies I see the silver. The shine that splits our worlds.

A shadow buzzes on to the surface. Two black wings spread out in a V. A gull. It gets bigger. Bigger. Closer.

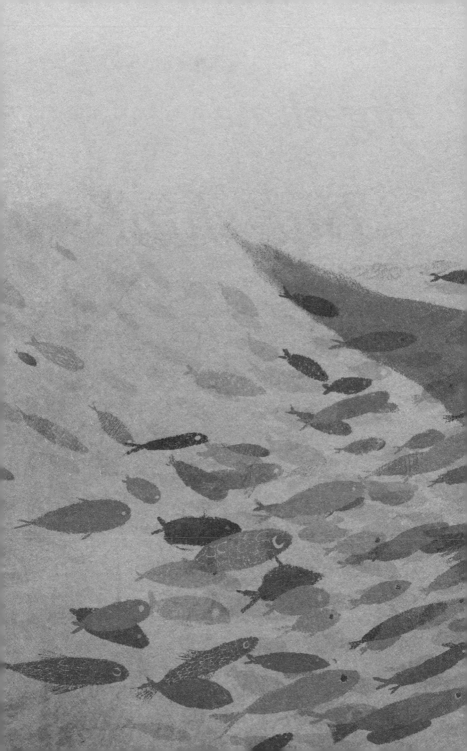

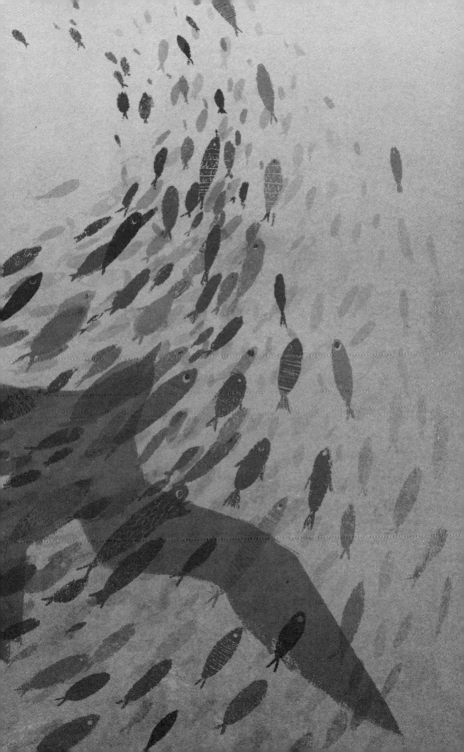

We shoot back down.

No, their heads shake and shiver.

Fast-dark, they say. We zigzag down. Twisting from every shadow. Avoiding imaginary *fast-darks*.

Hard-it

They shout and split into two. Round a rock.
Me and my fish shoot off left and meet back up on the other side.

Here

Here

Here

They clock back in as they join up. Their voices coiling round each other.

Us

Us

US

THIS?

They say and freeze. Sudden and sharp. They hang about, eyes flicking around. Freaking out.

I don't stop. I can't.

I would slam into the fish in front but they pop into a tunnel and I glide straight through, trying to stop. My hand slips off my mackerel. My arms and legs thrash about. I feel very pink and human.

My fish swims down. Straight down. Into a barnacle shelf rock and bounces off. The shoal flinches and draws back.

'*Ow*,' my fish says, like he's teaching a class of Year One's. He stots his tail off the rock and bounces back up. '*Ow*,' he says.

OW?

They look completely freaked out. Fish never touch anything.

The shoal look at each other, their heads and tails flicking together. '*Ow?*' they say.

Ow?

Then they start dive-bombing the rock.

Ow

OW

OW

They say.

OW

OW

OW

I roll on to my back and spin. Their singing fills me up. A laugh bubbles out my nose.

OW

OW

OW

They don't stop.

They'd better stop though or they'll knacker themselves. I feel a bit sick. And bad.

I swim down to the rock. They streak past me. Head first. Their shadows scoot over my skin. I cover it with my body. The shells scratch my hands. 'No ow,' I say. I shake my head. They freeze. Heads like arrows. One fish stops by my belly button.

'No ow,' I say.

I have no idea if they know what this means. I feel their eyes, dizzy and wonky, trying to stare at me. The sea creaks in the silence. I put my hands out.

NO

NO

No

They shake their heads and wiggle backwards. As one.

'Here,' I say and point away into the emptiness. 'Go,' I say.

This they get.

Go

Go

Go

I have a thousand echoes. My fish wriggles back under my hand. The shoal wraps back around us. I grin at him and we go. We fly into tails and blur.

I stick with the *Us*. Sharp diagonals and crazy turns. They read the water, the currents, the thermals. Sun bursts through to light up the grey, makes passages into the unknown.

They disappear into thick brown.

Soft-it

They shout. I buzz my belly on a patch of bladderwrack weed. It's a great *soft-it*.

'Right!' I shout.

Right

Right

Right

They say.

We don't go right. It doesn't mean anything to them. I laugh and get a mouthful of rainbow wrack weed. I spit it out.

'Left,' I say.

Left

Left

Left

They say.

We don't go left either.

We go down.

Suddenly there's a massive

YES

And we stop. I wish they would stop doing that. I bring my feet up just in time, bend my knees and bounce off a rock. It stings my toes.

I look back at a thousand expectant faces.

Ow?

They say, all of them.

I check my foot for blood. There is none. 'Yes. Ow,' I say and grin. They nod and wiggle.

I look around. I have no idea why we've stopped. They look so excited.

YES

They say. Like this means something to me. It doesn't.

'Yes?' I say.

They all fly past, into the rock. But not to ow, not this time. They're pecking at something I can't see. Moving back and forth, sucking something in. We've stopped for dinner.

My fish looks at me and nods. He pokes his nose into the 'food' to show me.

YES, he says

He looks so pleased. What else could I want?

I pretend to eat some. I imagine the microscopic copepods we're sucking up.

YES, he says.

YES?

'Yes,' I say. This is ridiculous.

He buries himself in with the others and tucks in.

YES
Yes, he says.

And the shoal joins in till the sea is one massive chorus of

YES

I look at them stuffing their faces.

I remember Patrick and his Doritos.

How long has he been there?

How long have I been here?

I have to go.

I tap my fish on the back. He flicks round.

I look at the tags. 'Megallas,' I say. 'Go.'

Go? he says.

No

He points his nose back at the food.

YES, he says.

'No,' I shake my head, point at my chest. 'Up. *Big-shine.*'

He looks so sad.

'Back,' I say. 'Tomorrow.'

I have no idea if fish have days. If they just have moon and sun and dark? I don't know.

'Back,' I say again. 'Tomorrow.' And I wave and kick up.

I look down.

His eyes follow me as I go.

I break the surface.

Hard-its

My lungs splutter into life. Like I'm a body switching over.

I suck air in and look for the shore. I have no idea what direction I'm facing.

I use my brain like migrating spiny lobsters, who trek in convoys to lay their eggs. I find my instinct and trust it.

I see the crocodile rocks. They're not close, but not too far either. I'm so buzzed up, I could swim anywhere. The sun's on the horizon. The light bounces off the glass of Tesco Extra at the top of town. I've got time. Just. Just enough before Mum and Dad start freaking out.

I try to remember the feeling of the fish. The

rhythm. The muscle. The way they read and rode the water. It feels wrong to be bobbing on the surface. Like I'm gonna get picked off by a *fast-dark*. Sir David says, 'The most sensitive parts of lobsters are their stomachs.' I dip my head with every stroke to be on the safe side.

I reach the shallows and walk through the waves and onto the sand. As soon as I step out the water I feel heavy. My feet sink up to my ankles. The water pulls them back and doesn't let go. I lift my leg and step out.

Patrick looks up from his *Zebracadabra* book. 'The magic comes from the hands of the magician,' he says, 'not the cards.' He pops a queen of hearts into his palm, waves his fingers and it is gone. He snaps the book shut. 'You look . . .'

'What?'

'Weird.'

'Oh.' I pick up his provisions kit and chuck it into the air. I have energy I don't know what to do with. Patrick keeps staring at me. I catch the bag. He shoves me. We fight over it on the sand. He wins and raises the fingers of steel. I pass it over.

'Your skin's sticky,' he says.

'It's the salt.'

'SO?'

'What?'

He elbows me in the stomach. 'Did it come back?' He does a fish face. 'What did it *SAY*?'

The street lights fuzz on orange. 'Yeah,' I say. 'He was there.' The insects of the night lift. I think about everything. It feels too big to say.

'What did it want?' He hits me on the head with the book.

'It's kind of hard to explain.' I stand up and rub the sand out of my hair.

'Oh.' He looks hurt. I feel bad.

We don't say anything for a bit.

He sits up and puts his arms around his knees. 'You wanna go cycling?'

'Now?'

'Tomorrow.'

'Okay.' I blow a daddy long legs away from my nose.

'Cool.'

I put my fist out. We bump knuckles. I think of the fish. A grin takes over my face. 'It was amazing,' I say and knuckle him on the shoulder. 'I think it was the most amazing thing I've ever done in my entire life.' Patrick smiles too and springs aces out of his sleeves.

We walk off. I look back at the waves coming in,

creeping up the sand. I wonder what my fish is doing right now. Without me.

We walk up the steps and on to the gravel with no shoes and my brain says:

Ow

Ow

Ow

There are many, many *hard-it*s.

The Most
Undiscovered Place
in the World

I sleep-walk home, sleep-eat dinner and try to get to sleep-sleep dreaming about the fish. All of them. I don't think about Mum. I don't think about the tests.

In the middle of the night I wake up. I don't know why. I get out of bed and open the window. The street is silent. I see the rooftops. Even the pigeons are asleep.

A cat jumps from a gutter and looks back up at me. Green eyes in the dark. We stare at each other. There's no wind. The cat slinks off down the street.

I hear the sea.

I want to be there. To be back in the *Us*.

I stand against the window ledge like a potoo bird,

who can blend perfectly into the shape of a tree.

Sir David walks past one in the Amazon Basin and says, 'The only thing that could give it away are its beak and its eyes.' As he passes it bends its head and closes its eyes to become a broken branch.

I shut mine and listen to the waves.

Human Rocket

Me and Patrick meet up at the top of Hope Street. Patrick has a Giant Escape Jr 24, I have a Flite Panic BMX. It's a bit small. I've had it since I was nine. It's got a gap on the handlebars where I took off the hamburger bell that Howard gave me.

We look down at our wrists.

'10.03,' we say and high-five the watch sync.

It's the kind of day that looks like it's thinking about getting hot. The sun hovers. A guy in red shoes walks by on his mobile and into a tree. He bounces off like he meant it and keeps going.

I look at Patrick. 'Where d'you wanna go?'

'I dunno, it's your town,' he says.

'It's your life,' I say.

'It's your death,' he says.

'What?'

'If you wanna follow.' He grins at me and scoots off up the street.

I stick my feet on the pedals and go after him. He's fast. He's really, *really* fast.

The trees at the edge of the pavement blur by.

We go down Murray Street, past the bungalow houses with plastic stencil flower windows and empty stubby rose bush gardens. Up past Shoe Right and Cut the Cr*p hairdressers where the hill starts. You can't go far round here without hitting a hill. My legs burn. I see Patrick like a fly disappearing into the distance. He does a left past Wok this Way, a right out of town and up. Left on to the small lanes. The cuts. He takes the corner fast, his knee goes out to the side. Like a pro.

I take the corner and break before I smash into the fence.

My handlebars are wet with sweat. My front wheel is in the ditch.

I pull my chin away from the barbed wire. Up here there's fields either side. Roads that no one uses any more cept bikers, joggers, tractors. The fields are full of corn stubble. Stalks left over from the harvesters. The Toro machines that suck up everything and spew it into massive trailers. Black fly are riding the thermals coming out my head. Patrick's disappearing up the next hill.

Sir David watches a springbok running from a leopard that's just lost its cover. 'He's blown it,' he says.

'WAIT!' I yell.

I don't think he's heard but he stops and turns round. 'WHAT?'

'PLEASE.'

He waits.

He swoops back down the road like an osprey, an Iranian eagle owl. Easy.

He stops. His brakes don't even squeak. I'm still getting my breath back. He isn't.

'All right?' he says.

'Yeah,' I say, 'kind of.' I wipe my sweat with the back of my hand. 'Nice bike.'

'Crystal Palace junior cycle cross champion.' He grins back at me. 'It's not about the bike.'

'Swap yer?' I say.

'Deal.'

I take a long drink from my water bottle. We swap. We go.

The bike is slick. I am still slow.

Patrick is a human rocket on mine.

We race up. The road dips after the top. We fly past the old farm, the outbuildings, the telescopic loader stacking pink wrapped bales. Past four houses, in the middle of nowhere, for no reason.

At the top of Stag Bank he slows enough for me to nearly catch him and glances back over his shoulder. 'Ready?' he says.

'For what?'

'This.'

He flicks right down a track. I follow through an open gate into a field. We bobble along through the cut down stalks like spring heads. The rattle goes through my hands and up to my shoulders. I'm desperate not to skid, to lose skin. The air rips past my ears. Patrick yells like an urban coyote, 'Yeee haaaaaaaw.'

I do a mountain lion. I'm grinning my head off.

We stop at the bottom and lean the bikes into the bale stack.

'Top speed 18mph, average 8.9.' He reads the bike computer. The one on the bike I've been riding.

'Is that good?'

'Nope.'

We climb up to the top of the bales. The plastic's hot from the sun. It smells sweet.

We look out over the town. Way below. So far away.

Cars snaking through. Houses on the streets filling up the cracks. Big, small, packed in, spread out. Our town is a kind of collage. The wind cools my head down. My legs are covered in dust.

'How d'you learn to do that?'

'Just cos I can't swim doesn't mean I'm crap at everything.' He headbutts me in the helmet. The plastic donks. I unclick mine.

We both point into the air.

'Falcon,' we say together.

'Jinx padlock.'

It's a draw.

The bird's shadow flickers on the stalk stumps.

Patrick pulls out a bag of revels and opens it with his teeth. We try to avoid the coffee ones. They melt on my hands before they reach my mouth.

'I'm not stupid.' He bites a small one in half. Orange. It's risky. It so easily could have been coffee. 'I still get it.'

'What?'

'Your fish thing.'

'Oh.' I take a malteser, they're so obvious and un-risky.

'I came back for you,' he says.

'When?'

140

'Just now.' He stares at me. 'I could've left you.' We both go for a raisin. 'You're slower than a Gila monster,' he says.

'A slug,' I say.

'A three-toed sloth,' he says.

I look down at the sea spreading out for miles, so big I just want to jump off the bales and right into it. I wonder what it must be like to have never felt that, to have never swum at all.

'I could teach you,' I say.

'You could just tell me,' he says.

I get a coffee and spit it over the edge. 'You'll think I'm nuts.'

'You are.'

'Cheers!' I take the last three minstrels, flop back on the plastic and tell him everything I remember.

Bob

'You have a pet shoal.' He rolls on to his side. 'That's so cool.'

'Actually I think they think I'm their pet. But they think I'm slow.'

'You are.'

I pull out a piece of straw from the bale and poke him with it. He eats the last revel.

'Technically, that's a YES,' I say.

'What do you call a fish with no eyes?' he says.

'What?'

'Fsh.'

'I think I might call him Nigel,' I say.

'Who?'

'Leader fish.' I sit up. 'I had a hamster called

Nigel. He died.'

'Hamsters die young.'

'He fell down the back of the radiator.'

'Oh. How about Sid?' he says.

'Pete?' I say. 'Sam?'

'Patrick 2?' he says.

I poke my piece of straw in and out his mouth. 'Star?'

'Star?'

'He's really shiny.'

'I don't know any boys called Star.' Patrick grabs my straw and chucks it. 'How about Ding? It sounds shiny.'

'Bob,' I say.

'Bob?' he says.

We sit there for a minute.

'Yeah. He's very, Bobby,' I say and a cabbage white flies past and seals the deal. Bob it is.

We stand up like the kings of the bales.

'You can teach them anything,' Patrick says.

'Maybe. They don't speak much really. They feel things. They're amazing.'

'Nature is amazing,' he yells.

'Houseflies hum in the key of F,' I say.

'Electric eels have enough electricity to kill a horse.'

He looks away. 'When are you going back in?'

'Tonight.' I squat on the edge. 'Coming?'

'Get your bike averages up and I'll think about it,' he says and we slide bounce down the bales. We slip at the bottom and into a thistle.

'Ow,' we say in our best Fish.

I try to pick the thorns out of my legs but they snap in my fingers. We climb back on the bikes.

'Go, trusty steed, go!' Patrick yells and we razz off, back up the bumps.

We properly bomb it down Stag Hill and have to stop at the bottom for a man and an arthritic Labrador standing in the middle of the road. The Labrador's legs are shaking. Its eyes are smiling. 'Sorry, lads,' the man says. 'He just doesn't have it in him any more.' We pat the dog's head. He lies down and wags his tail. We push our bikes round the side, careful not to bang his nose.

'How fast was that?'

Patrick checks the computer. '28mph,' he says.

'Cool.' I'm relieved.

He grins at me. 'But we can do better.'

Most of the way back is downhill. It's a good buzz. I stand up on the pedals. The air screams into my face. We do our best animal noises and sound ridiculous. But it's fun.

When we stop on Watson Corner my brake blocks smell of burning. We swap bikes back. Patrick goes and I wave and watch him overtake a Mini Cooper.

When I get in Mum comes down and looks at my sweat patches. I feel like a hag fish, producing slime.

'Nice ride?' she says.

'Patrick is the Crystal Palace junior cycle cross champion,' I say.

'Okay.' Her eyebrows look impressed.

We melt some butter and sugar in the microwave, stir in some oats and raisins and stick it in the oven to make flapjacks. We sit out the back on the grass and eat ham sandwiches and hot spoonfuls out of the tin. The sugar and the heat burn my gums.

'Billy . . .'

'Yeah?'

'You might wanna take a shower,' she says.

I shake my head. 'I'm swimming.'

'Now?'

'Yeah.' I prod my tongue into the bouncy bit of blister coming up in my mouth and run upstairs to get a towel.

'Back by eight, Billy, okay,' she yells.

'Okay,' I yell and am gone.

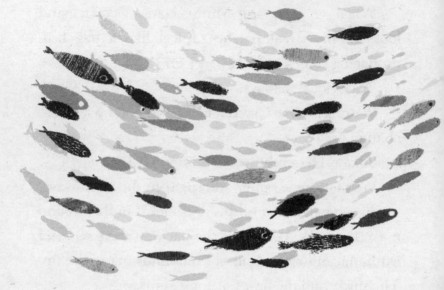

A Bit Weird

Halfy autumn wetsuit, check. Towel, check. Goggles, check. Out the back and past Zadie's . . .

Not check.

She surprises me with her head out the window. 'All right,' she shouts.

Music is blasting out.

'All right,' I shout back.

The wind blows the hair over our eyes and the music off the cliff.

I keep walking trying to look relaxed and trip over a pebble.

Me and Patrick meet up on the beach steps.

'*Rope Tricks in Five Ticks*.' He taps the book under his arm and winks.

'No provisions?'

'Not yet.' He pulls a head torch out of his pocket. 'Just this.'

It's Saturday, so the bay is busier. Lorraine from our street walks up the steps with Whisky their Scottie dog and Martha who's three. Martha stops and looks at Patrick. 'Uni Kitty dances on rainbows,' she says and holds up her horse, which hovers on a clam shell.

Whisky does a squat wee.

We step over it and go down. They go up.

'What you gonna teach them?' Patrick says. 'The fish.'

'I don't know.' We go over to the boulder side of the beach, out of the way of two kids with a kite. 'I just want to be there, y'know.' I climb up one rock and jump-step over the others. Arms out. 'You could teach them French,' he says. 'You could teach them anything.'

I put the towel down and spit into the goggles. 'What are you gonna do?'

'Read.'

'Okay.'

'And practice.' He pulls a piece of rope and a pair of scissors out of his pocket.

'Cool.'

'Okay. See ya in a bit,' I say. Neither of us knows whether to wave or not. So we don't.

'See ya,' he says and opens up his scissors and a packet of chocolate planets.

It all feels a bit weird. Like I'm invited to a party that he isn't.

I hop down off the rock. It's tricky but I manage it without falling or twisting my ankles and walk up to the water.

Us

I run in and dive under. The water looks bright and blue. The wind and the shrieks and the sounds disappear when I stick my head under. The sea sucks them all up. When my ears tink I know I've entered a different world.

'Hello,' I shout into the nothingness. 'I'm back.'

I swim out a bit. Past the small rocks to the big ledges. The creases and cracks and pillars where the sand stops. I watch a shoal of teenies just sitting in the swell.

I look up and see him coming. Zigzagging like a tail wag. Zipping through.

Fish Boy

Fish

Fish

BOY

Fish Boy

He's chanting like a song. He's my fish. I'm his boy. Somehow. He reaches my goggles.

He looks into my eyes.

'**Kesz**,' he says, his voice like echoes.

I put my hand on his back, ease out my lungs into gill mode. '*Kezdodik.*' I nod and we go.

We go low. Down over a barnacle ridge. Nose to nose with sea snails, hermit crabs, starfish. Two transparent shrimp prick their antennae and scoot off. I pull my thoughts into my body and make it over the ridge. Skin on.

We go up. Out into open water.

He swings me left. And right. I try to hold on. We go right again. It takes me a while to get it. Then I do. He's taking me walkies.

'Hey!' I yell and stop. Is my swimming not good enough? Do I need training? Makerel swim as 5.5 metres per second.

Okay. Fair enough.

'*Hey*,' he says and swims off.

I try to catch him and miss. He's like slippery soap.

151

'*Hey!*' He springs out by my elbow.

I wonder why fish can't laugh. I wonder if they can cry.

'*Us*,' he says.
Us
Go

He's about to drag us off. I put my hand out. 'Stop,' I say. 'No go.'

No?

He looks at me.

We bob about. My hair sticks out either side.

I want to teach him something, too. Like what?

I want to teach him his name.

I point at him. 'You,' I say. 'Bob.'

Bob?

'Yes!'

I point at me. 'Fish Boy.' I point at him. 'You Bob. Me Fish Boy.'

He looks totally blank. He darts into my armpit. '*Us*,' he says. '*Us*.'

I shake my head and point. 'You. Me.'

He swims into my neck and rubs up against it. '*Us*,' he says really quietly. If he had eyebrows I think they would be really sad ones.

'Okay, okay.' We're an Us or nothing. 'Us,' I say. '*US*,' he says and pops out again and drags us off to the twisting silver speck in the distance.

We're a good team. We weave thorough the water and fly in there, right into the shoal. A long stretchy mesh of flashes and twisting.

Bob takes me into the flow. I don't let go. I start to spin. One of the fish winks.

Fish Boy

Fish Boy

Boy

Fish

Fish Boy

Their voices come from up and down and all over. They thought flash me. I don't know what it means but I feel it from my rib to my ear bones.

'Round,' I say. 'Us.'

They nod. Thousands of heads.

Round

Go

Round

Us

We spin.

I think I'll feel kind of dizzy but I don't. I spin slowly at first. It feels nice. Then faster. I keep one hand on the tags.

Us

154

Us

                             Us

It's amazing. I flow into it.

Round and round. The water's stroking my forehead. I watch the patterns on their backs, the scales on their bellies and let them carry me. The land-world's so far away that I don't even think about it. I don't think about Mum or Dad or school or Patrick. I don't think about anything.

Soft-it

We spiral through kelp and weave back together.

Us

          Us

                    Us

It's so good to be in the *Us*.

Round

        Go

Round

Us

I'm grinning like mad, happy like a blown-up crisp bag. I don't want to burst. I don't want to be anywhere else. Ever. We flow, round and round. Is there anywhere else? I don't know.

Round

Go

Round

Us

One of them swipes a copepod off my foot. I start laughing.

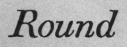

Round and round.
The rhythm of the water
wipes my brain clean. White.
Empty. Safe.
        The safeness of the *Us* is nice.
Seriously nice. The water blurs.
My hand loosens on the dog tags.
My arms float, soft and free. My
hair, my legs, my hands, my feet
flop out. I let everything go.

No

A chink of light bounces from the metal into my eyes. I open them and see the tags drifting up and away. I snatch them back down and shake my brain awake.

I think about Patrick. Waiting on the beach. For me.

I press the light on my watch: 7.03. I've been down here for two hours and twelve minutes.

I need to get back.

My head feels foggy. What was the word, what was the word? I can't remember anything. I start to panic, but the metal clanks on my chest. *Yeah right, look at the tags, dimbo*, I think.

'*Megallas*,' I say. The fish stop. Dead.

'Go.' I point at the surface.

Aaaaawwww

they say altogether, like a kid that's been told to switch off the TV. They're so loud I have to cover my ears.

Their bodies point at me.

No

Go

NO

They pull away.

I'm not in the *Us* any more. I am completely, totally, out of it. I'm bobbing about on my own.

'Sorry,' I try to say.

No

Go

NO

They chant. Bob turns to look at me. He gets nudged back into facing the front.

'Wait,' I say and reach out but I'm too late. They flick off into the grey.

WHAM!

The force of the flick pushes me back. My stomach sinks in. I curl my knees up into a ball. My lungs feel tight. I kick for the *big-shine*.

My face breaks the water and I gasp air in.

I'm with them or I'm not.

I'm not.

I look around and try to get some idea of where I am.

Sir David says, 'Even cataglyphis ants have to get back as quickly as possible to their nest to not risk death.' They live in the eastern Sahara and come out in the day when everything else dies. But they don't die. They navigate by the sun. They stop and turn and check and keep going.

I see the shore. Miles away. The sea is calm. The sun is almost down. The sky's gone bright pink. I breathe out and try not to panic. I take it one stroke at a time. I count twenty breaststroke dunks and look up. There's miles to go. A wave knocks me and goes into my mouth.

It feels hopeless.

I feel hopeless.

I wonder where Bob is.

I miss him.

The water's dark.

I stop swimming for a minute. I'm shaky cold.

I wonder how mackerel keep warm when they do not have fat. But they don't, do they. They're cold-blooded. They're not mammals. They don't feel anything the same as me.

160

Maybe I should have whale friends.

David A steps over the sand dunes and up to the screen and says, 'I think you should keep swimming.'

But I'm thinking of whales with shopping trolleys taking up the whole aisle of ASDA superstore. Buying freezers full of krill. Their trolleys start shoving into my back, nudging me out of the way. I try to sweep them off, but they won't go. I'm flowing along in the water, flying into hazy dreams. Floating in and out white space when my bum hits a rock.

I look down and see Bob swimming away.

No

Go

NO

He grumble chants off and doesn't look back.

I look up and see the shore.

He was my supermarket trolley. He has nudged me home.

A wave pushes me out and on to my feet. I bounce walk to the beach, pull myself up and go over to Patrick.

My body feels so heavy my legs are shaking. Patrick looks up from his *Rope Tricks in Five Ticks* book. His head torch stings my eyes.

He slams the book shut. BOOM.

I jump.

'Where were *you*?'

'Out. In. I d'know.'

He looks at his watch. '7.47,' he says. 'You've been down there for two hours and fifty-six minutes.'

'Hmmm.' My mouth is so cold it's kind of hard to move it properly.

'Your skin looks blue,' he says. I crumple down on to the sand next to him and he rubs my arms with the towel like I'm his little sister.

He kneels down and lifts up my eyelids. 'I think you're overexposed.' I don't even have the energy to lift my arm to dry my face. He feeds me chocolate planets.

I don't know how long we stay like that. I don't check my watch. It's totally dark when we walk back to my house. The stars are out. The wind is gone.

'Eat sugar,' he says on the back step. 'I'll be back tomorrow. Okay.' His face is orange in the street light. I nod and go in and upstairs and fall on to my bed and am asleep in the towel, before I have time to get under the covers.

Bed Slug

Monday.

Teacher Training Monday.

Get in.

I switch the lobster alarm off and go back to sleep.

At ten Dad comes in with French toast on a knee tray. The smell of hot butter comes up the stairs.

'Pellets for the bed slug,' he says and ruffles my hair. 'You were late last night.' He puts the trays down. I sit up.

'Was I?'

'Ooh toast.'

'Where were you?'

'With Patrick.'

'I don't even know Patrick.'

'He's coming round.'

'When?'

'Later.'

'Don't do it again, okay,' he breathes out.

'Okay,' I say. 'Sorry.'

We put cinnamon and icing sugar on with the sprinklers. I use the palm tree one, he has the love heart. When you take them off the toast it leaves the perfect shape underneath. Well, it does if your hand isn't shaking. Mine is a right mess.

'You okay?' Dad says, looking at my icing splodge.

'Yeah fine,' I say and shove the slice into my mouth. Dad raises an eyebrow.

We have two each and go down to the kitchen and I eat five more slices. We run out of eggs and go shopping. Without the van we have to walk. I take the black wheelie trolley, I'm not pulling the pink flamingos one. No way.

It's much easier getting there than it is getting back. The sun is boiling. My arms ache. I wish we hadn't bought so many beans. We sit on the wall by Loncar Lane to eat our Jive bars. I feel the heat soaked up in the bricks.

I break my bars in half, turn them into fangs.

'Nice one.' Dad sticks his up his nose.

164

'What's that meant to be?'

'I dunno.'

'A warthog?' I scan my brain. 'A wild boar?'

'The nose beast,' he says and roars. I laugh.

'You gonna eat those?' I watch him pull them out.

'Yeah.' He puts one in his mouth. 'Mmmn, salty.'

He wipes the chocolate off his nose with his hands, wipes his hands on his shorts. 'Fancy working on the Merz wall this afternoon?' We haven't done this for ages. I look at him and smile. 'Keep your eyes peeled on the way home then.' He gets up and looks over his shoulder. 'Race yer!' he says and legs it down the street. His carrier bags fly out, the pink flamingos trolley bounces over the slabs. I wish I could run. My arms feel like lead.

Part Gaudi, Part Kurt

Dad started the Merz wall in our back garden cos of this artist Kurt Schwitters. He's German but went to live in the Lake District where he made this art wall with all sorts of things in it. Nobody really liked his work while he was alive. Dad says this happens a lot with artists. I wonder if it'll happen with Dad.

He says our wall is part Gaudi, part Kurt. We collect things and stick them on with cement and pointy trowels. Sometimes the things mean something, like the ones we put on for birthdays, sometimes they're just beautiful, or interesting, sort of. Sometimes we make patterns, pushing whatever we've got into the cement and taking them out again. Shells, ferns, buttons, things like that. We make handprints every year. When I was seven I tried my nose but it didn't work.

Dad puts the shopping away and I stick my hands in the sink. I watch the water running over. There's a knock on the door.

'I'll go,' I say before Dad can. I wipe my hands on the front of my tiger shark T-shirt and open it.

'Hi,' Patrick says. We stand there for a minute.

Dad comes up behind me. 'How do,' he says and waves over my shoulder. We go into the kitchen. I pour us a Coke each and snap ice in. The three of us clink glasses. I like the way the outsides steam up. I write my name in mine. Patrick draws a fish and a question mark.

'So, what happened?' he whispers.

'Later,' I whisper back.

'We're doing the Merz wall,' I say in a loud voice so Dad can hear.

'Cool,' Patrick says, and shrugs. 'What's that?'

Making Merz

On the way home we found a safety pin, a stick shaped like a moustache, a white pebble and a bit off a necklace, a tiny silver heart. We go out and mix up the cement. I get some bits from the shed. It's dark inside and I have to stand still for a minute to get my eyes used to it, so I can see. Everything's covered in cobwebs. Dust flies up and sparkles in the light from the door. I get the tile crackers and a few old plates. I rub them on my T-shirt. One's got pink flowers on, the other an old picture of the queen, when she was really young. I get some tiles too and rub them till they shine, green, red and glitter blue. I make three piles by the wall and crack them up with the tac hammer.

Dad works over by the apple tree. I find a space at the other end. Patrick gets a patch next to mine by the rhubarb. I trace old parts of the wall with my fingers before I start. Each part flashes me back to the day we put it in and why. It's like a time machine.

I look at the ones Zadie put in. Ages ago. A Mickey Mouse car. A plastic fireman. Her tooth when it fell out in a pie.

Dad puts *Concerto De Arunquez* on and opens a window so we can hear the music outside.

'What do I do?' Patrick says.

'Just make it up.'

'Like animal shapes or something?'

'Like anything.' I use my hand to get the sun out of my eyes. 'It doesn't matter. Just do whatever you want.'

'The rules are, there are no rules,' Dad says and chucks him a trowel. I show him how to crack the tiles up into pieces with the tac hammer.

We don't talk while we work. We just scrape cement and stick. The patterns all flow out of our heads. Sometimes we stand back and just stare. We look at how the part we're working on fits in with everything else. Like cameras switching from close-up to wide angle. Sir David watches an orangutan washing socks in a river and says, 'The ability to imitate as well as to use

169

tools were ultimately to lead us to the transformation of the world.'

The cement dries fast. I have to keep pouring water over my head, down my back. My hands get dirty, so do Patrick's, so do Dad's. We don't use gloves. I watch the grey crack over my knuckles and feel it tighten on my skin.

At five we break for lemonade and cheese and pickle sandwiches. It feels like snapping out of the *Us*.

'Nice work,' Dad says and slaps Patrick on the back.

'Thanks,' he says, staring at the wall and nodding. He looks genuinely proud.

We go back to work till it's nearly dark. A moth buzzes past my face. They never know their own space, moths. The garden light clicks on and we jump.

'Had enough?' Dad says.

I look at Patrick. He nods. 'Okay,' I say.

'Sure thing, partner,' Dad says and does the Howard gun salute.

I pick up the leftover bits of tile. The snapped edges graze my skin. A trickle of red runs over the grey.

Patrick follows me into the shed.

'Where's your mum?'

'Resting.' I turn my back on him. I want my body

to put a full stop to that conversation. I pile the tiles on the shelves.

'Your dad's so cool,' he says. 'My dad would never let me do stuff like that.'

I think of his big posh house, his new car. 'Your dad's pretty loaded though.'

'So?'

'So? I'm just saying.'

He passes over more tiles. 'So what happened?' he says.

'When?'

'Well, duh!'

Dad sticks his head round the door. 'Ice cream?' he says. Perfect timing.

We sit with our backs to the opposite wall on the grass and look at our work. Me and Patrick have minty cones. Dad has a lager. I like the click and hiss of the ring pull. Not the smell that comes out after though.

'Where'd you put the heart?' Dad says.

'There,' I point next to the purple quartz.

'Nice.'

We sit watching the midges, the white fly, more moths, there's loads of moths. 160,000 different species. Sir David says, 'Death head hawk moths fly across the Mediterranean using the moon to hold their northward course.' The moth flies across Africa, over the Himalayas and into a beehive. 'Now the hungry traveller restores his energy before looking for potato plants upon which it will lay its eggs,' he says. The moth sticks its tongue into the honey.

I lick the mint.

We're a hot bank of bodies, warm against the wall, warm against each other. Dad puts his arm around me. I feel his fingers on my chest, they're not twitching any more.

'When Billy did that first one.' He points at the baby handprint. 'He cried his eyes out, didn't yer.'

'I was only like, one or something.'

'You wouldn't stop crying till we washed it off.' He holds my wrist up. 'Look at them now, hands like shovels.' Mine still looks small next to his. 'Nature calls.' He gets up. 'See yers in a bit,' he says and goes inside. It feels very quiet when he goes.

'I like your green bits,' I say.

'Thanks.'

'It looks like a labyrinth.'

'Does it?'

'Yeah, it looks like lots of passageways.' I tilt my

head to see the shapes, 'With no way out.'

'Oh,' Patrick bites the last of his cone, 'right. Yours looks like a mouth,' he says, pointing at my white patch. It looks silver in the moonlight. 'With teeth.'

'I thought it was a lobster,' I say.

'SO?' he throws his arms up. 'What happened?'

I take a breath. 'Weird stuff. Weird stuff happened.' I feel the dog tags nudging me under my T-shirt. 'He came back.'

'Bob?'

'Yeah.'

'And?'

'And, I said it.'

'*Kesz?*'

I think of how when you say a word loads of times it feels like it makes no sense anymore. Not that that one ever did. 'And he took me away. To the *Us*. And we went deep and it was nice and we went round and round and it felt . . . you know . . .'

'No. As a non swimmer, I have absolutely no idea.'

'Easy, like I didn't have to think about anything anymore . . .' I snap up stems of grass. 'Like everything was far away.'

'Oh,' he doesn't laugh, he just nods like he's thinking really hard about what I've said and I think he is probably the only person in the world who I could ever tell this to and also the only one who would ever believe it.

Why?

Monday. In science Mrs Jones draws a lifecycle of the mayfly diagram on the board in blue and red pen. We copy it into our books. *Egg, Nymph, Emerger, Adult, Spinner, Spent Spnner*. I don't know why we do this, why we don't just stick a photocopy of it in. That would be so much easier.

I look at Ben Nicholson's while he is sharpening his pencil. He does this every five seconds. His Spinner is perfect. He puts an arm across the page when he sees me. I look down at mine. The head is too big for the body and the legs are kind of limp. I think about rubbing it out but don't. I draw tiny hairs coming off the knees.

Jamie Watts walks over to the bin and bumps me.

My pencil shoots across the page. 'Aww sorry, mate, sorry,' he says. 'I just tripped yeah.'

The line goes straight through my Emerger's head, Oscar Pierce laughs. 'Sit,' Mrs Jones shouts and points at his empty chair. Ben Nicholson offers me one of his rubber collection.

I think of the oxpecker on the hide of the hippo, cleaning ticks out of the cracks. The hippo wades out into the swamp and the oxpecker hangs on. Sir David whispers, 'They have two toes pointing forwards and two backwards, so they can cling on at any angle, even on a slippery hippo.' The oxpecker flies off to get earwax off a zebra, dandruff off a giraffe. 'These partnerships between birds and other animals have become very beneficial,' he says.

I take the rubber from Ben and nod thanks. His eyebrows look sympathetic.

I look at the Emerger and think that living for just one day would be pretty good. Unless it was a bad one. But if it was a good day it could solve a lot of problems. I think of all the best things you could do in a day. Although you'd have to do them alone, unless you're a fast friend maker, which I am not.

According to the diagram though, all mayflies do is fly, eat and mate. I look over at Zadie. She sits two tables away from mine, next to Sarah Collins. They have identical purple pencil cases. Zadie is staring out of the window. Smiling at something. I can't see what. She has shaded her eggs light blue – they look very 3D.

The bell goes while I am still rubbing out. Oscar Pierce pretends to hold the door open for me when Mrs Jones is looking and then shuts it in my face when she isn't.

When I get out into the corridor Jamie Watts is taking Ben's PE shorts out of his bag. He chucks them to Oscar who chucks them back. 'Catch!' He throws them so they go into my face. I try to pass them back over to Ben but Oscar swipes them. He chucks them to Archie, who chucks them back to Jamie. Jamie throws them to other kids in the hall. It goes on like this for five more throws. Everyone's too scared not to join in with the gang. With the people *Us*. They won't stick out. Jamie Watts just stares at them. Do what I do or it'll be you next. No one ever says that but everyone knows it. I think of the angler fish. The bright bulb it dangles in front of its face. The massive teeth that hide behind it, that bite chunks out of anything that comes close.

Ben just leans against the wall and waits.

Jamie walks past him into the toilet, comes out and

blows his nose on my PE bag. Oscar and Archie laugh. Everyone else just looks away.

I go in to wash the bag in the sink. Ben fishes his shorts out of the toilet. I look at the floor and think of biting chunks out of Jamie.

Mrs Curtis sticks her head round the door. 'Everything okay?' she says. We look at each other, back at her and nod. Round the corner I hear Jamie Watts laughing. 'Outside!' Mrs Curtis shouts and I hear a door slam.

I stick my bag under the drier and go out. To the fall wall. Patrick's talking to Sheree. She walks away when I get there. 'What's she doing here?'

'Talking.' He shrugs.

'In our place?'

'It's just a place. Anyone could come here.' I think of him coming here with other people, people who aren't me. It feels like the ground is moving.

'She's always laughing at us,' I say. 'With Becky.'

'No she isn't.' Patrick tilts his head. 'They're probably just laughing about something else.'

'Like what?'

'How would I know?'

'I got you this.' I pull out a carrot from my bag. 'For the trick.'

He turns it over in his hands and sees the scared carrot face I've drawn on one end. 'Cool,' he says and smiles. I lead the way over to the chestnut tree at the far side of the field. Nobody goes there any more since someone scraped RABIES into the trunk with a pen knife. Melissa Hardy touched it for a dare and was off school for a week with shingles. Now everyone thinks it's kind of cursed. That it makes you get diseases.

I tell Patrick this while he's picking up conkers and nearly touches the tree by accident with his steely fingers. He just laughs and tries to poke it.

'Don't,' I say and grab his hand off. Just in case.

We play championship flicker, with beech nuts and stuff from under the trees. We play in three shot runs. I'm good with short sticks and beech nut cases, Patrick specialises in old conker shells. The shells are brown and wrinkled inside where they used to be smooth and white. I flick a conker – it goes about two centimetres. Patrick laughs and flicks a stick. It misfires and hits him in the eye.

My second shot get stopped by the first conker, but my third goes for miles. It hits Sheree. She picks it up and throws it back. 'A nut case for a nut case,' she shouts. The shot wins the run and we re-fuel ammo.

We stuff our pockets till they bulge. 'So what are you gonna do?' he says.

'About what?'

He makes a fish mouth, puffs his cheeks out.

'I don't know.' I turn a beech nut over in my hands.

'Are you going to go back in?'

'Maybe.' I strip some bark off a stick. 'It depends.'

'I wonder what they want. The fish. Why they picked you out in the first place?'

I shrug. 'I'm Fish Boy.' I look up at the tree. 'I'm one of them.'

We fiddle with our conkers.

'Billy,' he says.

'What?'

'Can I ask you something?'

I shrug. 'Fire away.'

'The question or the stick?' He laughs his donkey laugh. 'Your mum.' He lays down his best three in a line. 'Is something wrong with her?'

'No.'

'She sleeps a lot.'

'She doesn't.' I feel my face getting hot. I want to *Megallas* out of this conversation, fast. 'You don't know anything about her.'

'Okay.' He does a long haul with a paperclip.

180

'She seems nice.'

'She's not nice.' I lie down to aim. 'She's the best.' I ace the flick.

'Good shot,' he says and pulls a flier with his.

He looks at my hands. 'Billy.'

'Yeah.'

'I think you've run out of ammo,' he says and I look down at my finger flicking an empty space.

When

When I get back from school I get the key out from under the tap-dancing goose (Dad likes to rotate the key hunt options) and let myself in. I get the cheese puffs multipack out the crisps box and watch TV. Mum doesn't come down. I think about Bob. I wonder if he's waiting for me. I don't notice the bird calls slipping by in the kitchen.

The front door slams. Dad's footsteps go upstairs and come back down. He opens the door. 'Blummin' heck, Billy, what's all this?' He looks at the carpet. It's filled with empty cheese puffs bags. Sir David says, 'The sparrow hawk flies very fast and low and takes its victims by surprise.'

I look up. 'What?'

'Just . . .' He runs his hand through his hair. 'Clean it up, all right.'

I lick the orange off my fingers and pick the packets off the floor. They stick a little where I licked them. I get bean juice on my hand from the bin. I lick it off.

Nice?

No nice

No

No

I stick my tongue in the sink.

Dad switches the radio on. It says something about budget cuts. 'Champion.' He rolls his eyes and switches it off again. 'Beans?' he says and takes a tin out.

'Can't we have fish and chips or something?'

'Make mine a butter chicken with a garlic naan and mushroom pilau.'

'Really?'

'I wish,' he says and rattles in the drawer for the tin opener. I watch the tin spinning as he opens it. A little line of paper peels off the top.

'When's Mum coming down?'

'She's not.'

'What? Why? I thought she was getting better.'

He holds up his hands. 'I'm just the messenger,' he says. 'Maybe later, eh.' He pours the beans into a pan.

I go upstairs, into their room. Mum's got the covers pulled up and I can't see her face. 'Dad says you're not coming down,' I say and sit on the bed.

'Hmmn.' She pulls the covers higher. 'Not today, Billy.' Her voice is small.

'Why?'

'I'm not in the mood.' She pulls the duvet over her head.

I feel the sheets shake and peer in over the top. I think of how we used to play moles in there, when I was little. How it felt like we were at the centre of the earth, away from everything. I see Mum's crying. I don't know what to do. I stroke her back like we learned in massage class with Mrs McQueen. The way we'd rub each other's shoulders before RE.

'I'm so tired,' she's murmuring all quiet. 'I'm tired of being tired.' She wipes her nose with the back of her hand.

Dad comes in with a mug of tea. 'Hey.' He puts it down and climbs on to the bed, takes her head to his chest. 'It's okay, it'll all be okay.'

'When?' she says. 'When's that gonna be then?'

He breathes out a big long breath. 'As long as it takes,' he says. 'Anyway, we're not going anywhere, are we, Billy.' He winks at me. 'We're not going anywhere at all.' He puts his other arm around me and I put both of mine round Mum and lie with my head on her shoulder. 'So you're stuck with us,' he says, 'till you get wrinkly.'

'Really wrinkly.'

'Yeah, like a raisin.'

'Like a Dogue de Bordeaux,' I say.

'A what?'

'A dog, a big wrinkly dog.' I think of them getting old, me getting old. It's too weird.

'Yeah, like a wrinkly French dog.' Dad strokes her ear. 'But without the ears.'

'I like the big floppy ears,' she says and smiles.

'All right then, we'll save up for plastic surgery, for an ear transplant.'

'Remember that Alsatian? On Brook Hill,' she says. 'The one that used to bark up at the gate.'

'Miso,' I say. 'Miso Angry. It was a Japanese fighting dog.' Dad gave it the nickname. He used to bark right back at it and it used to shut up and run away.

'The blackberries will be coming out now,' she says and sighs. 'I used to love that walk.' She puts her head back down on the pillow. 'I can't go on like this,' she says really quietly.

'When the tests come back,' Dad says. 'It'll be better when we know what we're dealing with.'

I think of the Bermuda Triangle. How knowing it's called that never helped anyone, how it made no difference at all. The idea of giving it a name makes it feel like it'll never go away, like it'll be there forever. I just want it to disappear. *Go away*, I yell inside, *leave her alone*, as if it's a thing I can push out just by thinking.

My face screws up.

'You okay?' Mum says and strokes my hair.

'Fine,' I say and wipe my eye with the back of my hand and we all lie there in this big soggy heap, like blind mole rats, a big hot heap of rats in a hole.

DC-3 Flight NC-16002, 1948

On December 28th, 1948, pilot Captain Robert Lindquist of Flight NC-16002 was flying from San Juan in Puerto Rico to Miami, Florida.

When he was fifty miles away Captain Robert Lindquist radioed the Miami control tower. He asked for landing instructions. Miami radioed back with instructions. They got no reply. Reports state that there was no radio trouble and the weather was clear. The plane never arrived at Miami and Flight NC-16002 was never heard from again.

Surprise

When I get back home the next day Mum's all bright eyed. Her best friend Leslie comes out of the bathroom with hands the colour of school toilet block.

'What d'you think?' Mum flaps a bit of hair over her shoulder.

'It looks nice.' I tilt my head sideways.

'Starry Night Blue Black,' Leslie shouts over the banister and twiddles her inky fingers. She comes down and pours tomato soup out into two bowls and puts her coat on.

'You not stopping?' Mum says.

'Nah, I've got a date with a nailbrush.' She hugs Mum, waves and leaves. I stir the soup, checking for any bits of blue. I get a tissue and wipe a thumbprint off the side of the bowl.

'Dad's coming home early,' Mum says stirring hers, 'with a surprise.'

'A surprise? Like what?'

'Beats me.' She gets up to butter the not-burnt toast. I see she's been drawing a picture in a sketch pad on the table. She sees me looking and flips it shut. 'I'm a bit out of practice,' she says and pulls a face.

I open the pad back up. 'It looks good,' I say even though the seagulls are a bit wonky, the wrong size for the mountains.

'Ta anyway,' she says and ruffles my hair. I think of all the things a surprise could be. A dog? A car? Chicken chow mein?

I hear Dad's keys in the lock and he springs in through the door.

'What is it?' I put my spoon down in the soup and the handle slides under. I rush over to see what he's got. He hasn't got anything.

'What it is, is the solution. What it is, is movement, freedom, us lot together again in the wild blue yonder.'

'A new van?' I say.

'A holiday?' Mum says.

'Better,' Dad says and taps the side of his nose and won't tell us anything else, not even when I tickle him in his underarm weak spot. He just chucks me on the sofa and arm chainsaws me until I shout 'Mercy'. The doorbell goes and we jump up.

'I'll get it!' Dad shouts and runs over. There's someone there in a white shirt with a badge that says Nina and a big red cross underneath.

'Mr Shiel,' she says.

'That's the geezer,' Dad says.

'Pardon?'

'Yes,' says Mum. 'He means yes, it's him.'

'We've got a delivery for you.'

'Bingo,' says Dad. 'Great stuff.'

'If you can just sign here.' Nina gives him a clipboard.

'Shouldn't I write my name instead?' She looks back at him, blank. 'Instead of *here*?' he says.

'Just sign it, Dan,' Mum says.

I look round the side of them and see a big white van outside, a really good one. Nina goes to open the van door, Dad goes down the steps after her. 'I'll give you a hand,' he says. 'In fact, I'll give you two.' He waves both hands.

I kind of want Dad to shut up. I think Mum does too as she folds her arms and rolls her eyes. We wait for the surprise. Nina unlocks the van door. The surprise isn't the van – it comes *out* of the van. Dad carries it up the steps. It isn't anything I was thinking of. When I see it I wish I hadn't. My heart thumps down into my shoes.

'Ta-da!' Dad pushes the sides to open it up, to make the seat.

'It's a wheelchair,' Mum says.

'It's your passport to the outside world,' Dad says.

I don't know what to say. Inside I'm screaming *NO WAY, I don't want my mum in that!* I feel like everyone will look at us and feel sorry for us, like it'll make what's inside outside, so everyone can see and I don't want them to, I don't want them to see her that way.

'We can go everywhere, just like we used to,' Dad says.

'It's great,' Mum says and looks like she's going to cry.

'What's up?'

'It's all right.' Mum wipes her nose with her sleeve.

'It isn't.' He puts his arm round her and she leans into his chest.

'It won't be like it used to be, cos I'm not. Am I. Things can't be, you know . . .'

'I know,' he says. 'I know. But you can get out can't you and Billy can help. He's a big strong lad, aren't yer,

Billy. You'll help Mum won't you.'

I just stand there looking at the wheelchair on the step like it's an alien come into our world, like when an ant comes to join a colony and they have to decide if they want it to or not, if it's going to be part of them or they're going to send it away or eat it.

Dark clouds gather in my brain and Sir David says, 'Since life began around four thousand million years ago it has gone through some extraordinary changes in its climate. You and I belong to the most widespread and dominant animal on earth. The fact is that man has unprecedented control over the earth and everything in it and so whether he likes it or not, what happens next is very largely up to him.'

I feel the storm stirring inside me. I see the wind sweeping over the Atlantic cranking itself up, sucking moisture and twisting, reaching a hundred miles an hour, a hundred and fifty, round and round, getting ready to go inland, to find its way out over the sea. I see Sir David open his mouth like he's about to speak. But he doesn't. My head buzzes. And then there's just nothing, just silence, like the screen's flicked off and David's face fades out into darkness.

He is gone.

The King of Hearts

We're in PSHE. Mr Norbund is trying to talk about third world child labour and his head is sweating.

'Terrible isn't it, sir.' Jamie Watts says. 'Nightmare.' He winks at Oscar and sticks two fingers up behind his back, so it gives him horns on the overhead projector.

Mr Norbund rubs his head with a white handkerchief and puts a DVD in the machine. It doesn't work. 'Ah.' He says and scrubs his head harder. 'A little help, someone? Anyone?' Robert Brentwood presses some buttons. The screen goes from blue to black and we watch a programme about sweatshops in India. It's actually horrible. Kids make trainers all day every day and earn like £15 a month. I totally had no idea. I look at them sitting on a concrete floor, squinting, sewing. I look over at Jamie's feet under the table. At the Nikes. I feel a bit sick.

*

When I go outside Patrick is talking to Robert Daynard and Joel Harris by the fall wall. I sit on the wall waiting for them to go away and watch Zonky fall off on to his knees. Blood starts to soak through his trousers, except that they are black. So the blood just looks like black on black, like marmite on burnt toast. You just sort of know it's there.

Joel does an impression of Mr Norbund. 'Someone, anyone.' It sounds exactly like him. Robert and Patrick laugh. I bite my cheek so I don't. Robert and Joel go to the canteen. 'Catch you later,' Patrick says and makes foam balls appear in their hands.

'Cool,' Robert says. Joel puts them in his eyes as if he's got zombie eyeballs. They throw them back. Patrick catches them and opens his hands, to show that they've disappeared. They turn and wave. I stare at Patrick. The look is meant to say *whose friend are you anyway?*

'Watch this,' he says and takes out his card deck from his shirt pocket. I think that Patrick is seriously not good at reading eyebrows. He pulls up on to the wall. His pocket stays square where the cards have been.

'Pick a card,' he says and fans them out.

'I've been thinking,' I say.

'Any card,' he says.

'About why.'

He puts them right up by my eyes so I can't see. 'A-n-y c-a-r-d,' he says really slowly. Sheree and Becky look over. I pick a card and hold it in front of my face. It's the king of hearts. 'Put it on the bottom of the pack,' he says, 'and slide the pack back in the packet.'

'You mean the deck,' I say. 'Slide the deck back in the packet.'

'Whatever,' he says. 'Make sure I can't see it.'

'How would I know if you can see it? You might have mirrors up your sleeves.'

'You want to check?' He holds his wrists up.

'No.' I slide the deck back in the pack.

'Okay,' he says and places the pack on his face. He starts slamming it into his forehead. 'What are you doing?'

'Imprinting your card on my brain,' he says and slams it into his head again. He makes the *Psycho* noise each time he bangs. 'Ree ree ree ree.' I try not to laugh but can't help it. He starts laughing too and blinks each time he bangs.

'Okay okay, stop,' I say. There's a pink mark on his head.

'Your card was . . .' He closes his eyes. 'The king of hearts,' he says and opens them.

I pull out his cuffs and look down his sleeves. No mirrors. 'What if it wasn't?'

'I know it was.' He puts the deck back in his pocket and fastens the button over.

'You're crazy,' I say and elbow him. He nearly falls off the wall. He elbows me back. We both stop when Jamie Watts and Oscar walk by.

Their shadows spread up the concrete.

Fast-dark

Fast-dark

There's nowhere to go. Jamie kicks a rock, I pull back and it misses my head by millimetres. We both look at the grass where it lands. Oscar makes his hands into a bra and pogoes past us. Random. We look at him. We look away.

'So, you were thinking,' Patrick says.

'Yeah.'

'So?'

'Maybe they just want company?'

'Who?'

'The fish.' I kick my heels against the wall.

'Right.' He cocks his head. 'I thought you said there were hundreds of them.'

'Different sort of company.'

'Human flesh?'

'No.' Since *the surprise* I have been practising how this would go. This is not how I thought it would go. 'Maybe I should go back in to find out.' I try to sound casual.

'Really?' He sings the *Jaws* tune. Duh dut duh dut duh dut.

'If I don't I'll spend my whole life wishing I had.'

'Not if you're dead,' he says. 'If you're dead you'll spend your very short life wishing you hadn't.'

'It's safe, okay.'

He looks at me.

'That's why they have shoals.' I poke him in the card deck. 'It keeps them safe.'

'They have shoals so one of the others gets eaten not them,' he says.

'They don't.'

'They do.' He breathes out. 'When?' he says.

'Tonight,' I say. 'We can camp out.'

'You want me sit on the beach *at night*? *Alone?*'

197

'No, well, yes. I dunno. Maybe. Everyone does it. In the summer.' I shrug. I hadn't really thought this far. 'I can bring cheesy Doritos and a torch. You can read your rope book. Please.'

'The *Self-working Rope Magic* book.' He scratches the back of his neck. I feel the breeze lift. It flicks back his fringe. 'Just for one night?'

'With a bag of Doritos,' I say. 'A family-size bag.'

'Okay,' he says and rubs his neck again. 'Just once.'

Portal

I get out my old Mystery Machine money tin and try to pull the stopper out the bottom. It doesn't budge. I get the swordfish knife out of the kitchen drawer and push the corner till it pops.

POP

SMASH

The coins fall out on to the worktop. I slide them into rows with two fingers. Two pounds fifty-eight. It should be enough. I pull all the coins over the edge and into my pocket like the 2p slot machines with things you never win. 'Jackpot,' I say.

When I open the front door the wind blows it out of my hand and into the wall. WHAM. I cling on to the handle, step on to the street and lean right back to pull it shut. The change bulges in my pocket. I jingle off to John's Corner Shop.

BING BONG. The door beeps.

The cheesy Doritos are on the wall of crisps, right of the Stackers, left of the Monster Munch. I look at the pyramid of Toblerones and think how the door beep is like entering a portal to another world. I put the packet down on the counter. John is arranging the chocolate saws and mini fried eggs display. 'Lime-filled chocolate skull?' He picks one up out of the tray. It is white chocolate with green eyes.

'Just these thanks,' I say.

He wipes his hands on a checked cloth behind the till. I pull the money out of my pocket and on to the counter. 'Phew, really raided the humbug for this one, eh?'

'Humbug?'

'Mint,' he says and laughs his chest rattler laugh. 'Raided the mint.' His eyebrows are so hopeful I try to laugh too.

'Good one,' I say.

John would smile even if attacked by a boxing kangaroo. 'Okey dokey, down to business,' he says and stops laughing and starts counting. He looks like he's really concentrating. A girl with Heelys comes in, picks up a Crunchie and rolls for the door. 'Fifty-five pence,' John says holding a hand out, without taking his eyes off the counting for a second. He's a pro. She pays up and leaves.

'How's that lovely mum of yours?' he says without looking up.

'Fine.'

'And your most delightful and energeticful father?'

'Fine.'

'And your most excellent dog?'

'I don't have a dog.'

'Right.' He slams the till draw and it dings.

'One pence over,' he says, handing me it back. 'The boxes are building up you know, eh.' He points to the pile of chocolate kittens' tongues. It is very large and slopey. On the boxes there's these rows of teeny tabby kittens and gold loopy writing that says Katzenzungen. They're Mum's favourite. She says she likes to support a little bit of bonkers. She's the only one who ever buys them.

'Sorry.' I shrug and take the crisps.

'Hey, Billy, catch,' he says and throws me a sherbet cola bottle. 'To keep you fizzy,' he says.

'Fizzy?'

'Rhymes with busy?' He waves his hand as if

chucking the joke over his shoulder. 'Ah, I'm working on it,' he says.

'Ta,' I say and wave and feel very flat.

The door beeps as I leave and the portal bubble bursts. When I look back John is already restocking the empty crisp space. I think of Dad pushing Mum round here, everybody seeing, staring. How we'd have to park the wheelchair outside. How everyone would know.

I think of the floor of the rainforest. A camera zooms in on the burrow of a jewel wasp. Sir David isn't there, not any more. I can't see him at all. It's like a TV where the screen doesn't work. I hear his voice, but I can't see him. My stomach jolts. It's weird.

'Here she lays her eggs directly on to the cockroach and covers the tunnel with leaf litter. The larvae spend five days sucking the cockroach's bodily fluids then they will burrow inside and begin to feed on the nervous and breathing system. All the time the cockroach is alive and powerless to respond.' The cola bottle feels slimy in my mouth. I spit it down the drain, grip the crisps tighter than I mean to and go home.

Can't or Won't

When I get back, the wind is rattling the windows in the kitchen like it's trying to break in. I get out my Quickpitch Compact Tent, my Wilderness sleeping bag and LED Lenser X21 Xtreme torch and stuff them into one of the big blue IKEA bags by the washing machine. In the fridge there's half a pack of frankfurters. I stick them in too and get a disposable BBQ from the cupboard under the sink and rub the cobwebs off with my sleeve. The Doritos go on top to stop them getting any more squashed.

I write *Gone camping with Patrick. Back tomorrow* on the back of a red EDF envelope on the table and slide the note under a bean tin to kind of let on it's a camping/swimming combo.

The clock makes the sound of a warbler. I swing the bag over my shoulder and am about to open the door when someone else opens it first. The air gasps in like it's been dying to for ages, like it's been holding its breath.

The someone else is Dad. He looks hot, like he's run home. I step back. My note flutters under the bean tin. He shoulders the door shut. He looks at me, at my towel. 'Oh,' he says, 'what you up to?'

'I'm going to the *Us*.'

'What?'

'Out. I'm going out with Patrick. Tonight.'

'You never asked.'

'I thought it'd be all right.'

'Well it isn't.' He breathes out. 'I thought we were going for a walk.' He points at the wheelchair. 'All of us. *Together*.'

'Sorry,' I say and look at the floor. I don't look at his eyebrows. 'It's important.'

'*This* is important, this is your mum,' he says. 'I thought you cared.'

'I do.'

'I thought you were bothered.'

'I am.'

'Well it doesn't look like it Billy, does it.' He slams a

hand on the worktop. 'Are you coming or what?'

'I can't.' I want to tell him about the fish, about everything, but I don't.

'Can't or won't?'

I pick a thread loose on the towel.

Mum pushes the kitchen door and the window blasts open, BHAM. We all jump. The wind rips three of Dad's tea towels off the wall. I try to shut it but I can't quite reach. Mum's hair blows back from her face. She walks over to the sink, reaches up and clicks it shut. Dad picks the tea towels up off the floor.

Mum looks at him, looks at me. 'Everything okay?' She tips her head to one side. Dad brushes the tea towels flat with the back of his hand. He looks up and puts a smile on quick. 'We've got a date,' he says, 'you and me.' He holds an arm out for her to loop through. 'Fancy taking a turn?'

'Don't mind if I do,' she says.

'Your chariot awaits . . .' He goes to get the wheelchair ready.

'See you then,' I say.

'In by ten, right. Tonight.' Dad says and doesn't look back, not at me, not at all.

The FDT

I walk down the coast path and kick stones over the edge. They clunk down, smashing on the rocks. It's cold. And grey. The wind is going crazy.

I walk past Zadie's. She sticks her head out the window.

'Hey, Billy.'

She looks at my face. 'You all right?'

'No.'

'Wait!'

I just keep walking.

The air blasts into my knees, my back. I have to keep stopping, to change arms. The bag is so heavy it leaves red stripes on my shoulders. The wind lifts it and smacks my knuckles into my face. I drop the bag

206

down on the bench and feel the heat on my cheek, where it hit. I lean right into the wind, up on my toes, see how far out I can go. It holds me up like a giant hand, pressing into my chest. *Come on then*, I think, *bring it on*, as if I'm calling it in from the sea. I look down at the rocks. It could change direction and let me go, it could drop me down there in a second. I shake my head and pull myself back.

I pick the bag back up and look at the bench. No one ever sits here because of the wind. It's got a plaque on it that says '*IN MEMORY OF MR AND MRS E WHO REALLY LOVED THIS SPOT*' and I wonder who they were and why they didn't mind the wind. Or if the bench people put it up in the wrong place and if their ghosts are hanging around in a beautiful non-windy place waiting to rest in peace.

I walk down the steps. The wind kicks the beach up and sandpapers my face. It's a fine to medium grit gauge today (£2.29 a square from Bang and Blast). I think of Dad. I think of Mum. I think of them together. Out. Lost in their own world without me.

I meet Patrick at the bottom. He's got an Army Surplus rucksack on, everything neatly packed. His shoulders look fine. We climb up the needle paths into the dunes. We go over, into a moon crater and rest our backs against the sand. Our hair drops down, back on to our heads.

We set up camp at the crater base, in the bowl. The wind tries to whip in round the edges. Popping the tent up is easy. Pegging it out isn't. We put rocks on top of the pegs to try and keep them in.

'What if it blows away?' he says.

'It won't if you stay in it.' I bang a rock on the last peg.

'Thanks.'

'Actually it would be pretty cool sea surfing in a tent.'

'Yeah, if you can *swim*.'

I keep forgetting he can't. 'It's cheaper than easyJet,' I say.

'It probably isn't,' he says, 'and I kind of prefer arriving places actually alive.' He puts on a BIG rock. 'Anyway I have to be back by ten.'

'What?'

'House rules.' He pulls a face.

'Same.'

I leave my leg out to trip Patrick over as he goes by. He does a proper comedy fall and headbutts the sand. It's very funny until he throws a handful of it in my face. He knocks me down and stands over my head with two handfuls ready loaded. 'Peace,' I say. 'Peace.' He backs away and I wipe it off and feel like all my skin is scraping off too.

We light the instant BBQ with Patrick's flint and steel and cook the frankfurters. We poke them with sticks because we both forgot forks and they burn in like two seconds. I eat mine off the stick. It's a bit black but still hot and delicious. I burn a bit of my gum. We swig Patrick's Dandelion and Burdock out of the bottle.

The BBQ lasts for ages. We try heating up Doritos but they taste a bit strange. We keep our hands warm on it as the sun goes down. I take my trousers and shirt off.

'How long will you be?' he says.

'I don't know.' I jump up and down, trying to get my full-length wetsuit up my legs. I haven't worn it for ages. I wonder if I'll be able to get it off again. I stretch on my swim shoes.

'Three hours? Four? Six?'

'Does it matter?'

'I need to know the FDT,' he says. I give him the *what does that even mean* look. 'The Friend might be Drowning and needs help Time.'

'Oh.' I think maybe he is a better eyebrow reader than I thought. 'Shouldn't that be the FMBDANHT?'

He sticks two fingers up at me. I jump on him and we roll around in the sand for a bit. I stand up and dust sand off my elbows. 'I'll be back in three,' I say.

'Have you got your tags on?'

'What are you, my mother?' I say and jingle them under his nose. I don't tell him that I always have them on. Even in the shower.

'Okay, okay.' He swats me away and I fall over in the couch grass and yelp when the stems stab my hands. He looks down at his feet, up at me.

'Take this.' He passes something from the palm of his hand to mine. It's hot from the heat of him.

'What's that?' I open my hand out.

'What d'you think?'

I look at the metal, the hole in the top. I see my face bending in it. My big nose as I pull it closer. It's a whistle. 'What for?'

'Just . . .' He puts his hand in his pockets and shrugs, 'in case.'

Of what? I think but don't ask. I loop it over my neck and down my suit. 'Race yer,' I say and we run back up to the top of the ridge. At the top the wind blast nearly knocks us over. We cling to each other's elbows to get our balance. Then we let go.

'Billy.' Patrick turns to look at me. 'What if you

don't come back?'

I keep staring straight on. 'What?'

'What if you don't. What if you don't want to?'

We look out at the waves. I think of the underneath, the stillness, the spinning, the miles away from everythingness, the nothing. The *Us*.

'What if you can't?' he says.

Megallas, I think. I rattle the code word around in my head. *Megallas, Megallas*. I try to drill it in there. Just in case.

'I will,' I say and don't look back at him. I step out down the needle path, my arms folded, fingers crossed. 'I will,' I shout and kamikaze it down the sand to the bottom.

Gone

I walk down the beach, squint as the sand blows up into my face. Even the cliff's shoulders can't hold it off today.

Sir David's in the Arctic watching a fox leap for lemmings. But I still can't see him. It's just all snow and ice and nothing. Just a voice from nowhere. 'It's a meagre existence,' the voice says, 'and the worst of winter is yet to come.' The fox misjudges a leap and gets its head stuck. 'Adolescence for an Arctic fox is nearly always a solitary journey. The only way of surviving is to split up and face the six-month-long winter alone. Even so, a young fox has only a one in five chance of surviving.'

I think of Mum.

What if you don't come back? I hear Patrick's voice in my head. I push it out. It doesn't matter right now. It's the going out that matters. The spray blows up around my ankles. I walk out into the surf and dive in.

I stick my head under the water. The swell pulls and pushes the sand underneath into clouds. The sea seeps into my suit, I shudder till it warms up. My breath bubbles round my ears. Sea water's heavy, it's not like swimming pools, it's thick and muckle and strong. Blowing out is harder.

I look for Bob. It feels weird in the dusk. The wind's making the water angry today. Pieces of weed and green and brown and froth and mush are ripped up and chucked around. It's hard to see. I try to stop bits blasting into my mouth and push them away from my face.

He isn't here.

The water pushes me about.

I swim out.

I keep pulling away from the rocks the waves keep trying to push me into. I tuck my knees up and roll myself into a hermit crab ball to miss a boulder. The water pulls me back and I spring out, arms and legs clawing away like a polar bear.

I feel out of it up on the surface: the *Us* happening

213

down there without me.

I stick my face under the water. '*Ketsz*,' I shout, '*kezdodik*.' I think of how whales can hear each other from miles away, how seals sense vibrations in their whiskers. I feel like my voice is turned into waves, trapped up in pockets of air, not words any more, just a feeling, just something you can sense, that you can tune into. Or not.

I wait and watch. Nothing. I shut my eyes. *Come on*, I say in my head like they can hear it through the water. *Come on*. I let my thought waves flow out. I think of how lightning can be everywhere at once.

I open my eyes and see something, so far off it's hard to be sure, like a candle, a tiny flickering flame. I keep watching. It could be a can, a piece of net, rock, sand, anything. But I know it isn't. The tiny silver dart heads my way. Never in a straight line. Flick, flick, flick. *I am Fish Boy*, I think, *he's come for me*.

Bob swims up to my knee and stops. I duck down further, to get my head nearer. My dog tags bounce out. He looks at the tags, then away, then back at the tags. I pull them into my hand and hold on tight.

'Hi,' I say. I wonder if I have hurt his feelings.

Go

214

Big-shine

No, he says.

I try to explain.

'Friend. Patrick. *Pink-fish.*'

Cept Patrick can't swim. He's not fish. He's just legs in *big-shine.*

Pink-fish?

His head looks over my shoulder, like the *pink-fish* might be there.

'Patrick,' I say.

NO

Pink-fish
NO

He says and shakes his head like a two-year-old.

Then he swims off to eat something off the rock. I think he's jealous. He swims back under my arm. I duck out the way of a flying mussel shell and put my fingers near his back.

I hover.

I think about swimming home and getting out. Like there's something wrong, something I can sense in my whiskers.

But I don't.

215

I put my hand on his back and we go.

We swim out into the gloom. It's thicker than last time. And bumpy.

Riding the storm is hard. Really, really hard.

We go deeper this time, further. I see the spinning, twisting speck of silver. It looks far away. He pulls. I try to focus. We have to turn faster to ride the currents. I bang my knees and elbows. I'm grateful for the full wetsuit.

He keeps looking back at me and saying,

Pink-fish

NO

I don't know why he's so bothered.

A beam of moon cuts through the water. We stop.

We look up at the light. Bits and scraps and stuff drift in and out and sparkle.

'*Sea-caller*,' he whispers. '*Sea-caller*.' He looks like he's seen a ghost.

We float there. We say nothing.

The light goes again and so do we.

The shoal looks beautiful in the dark, like a slice of stars, glowing out.

The moon comes back. It reaches its arm down into the water. A long, white light. The fish stop and stare and look up.

Sea-caller

Sea-caller

They wriggle float in the beam.

The light disappears and they snap out of it.

I swim over to the shoal.

Some of the mackerel nod at me; most of them turn away, as if they don't notice I'm here. A small one slips by my hair and says '*hi*' really quietly. I get the general feeling they're in a huff. I look down. Bob disappears. I turn around, look between my legs. I can't see him anywhere.

I try to get in the spin. The fish squeeze together and bounce me out. I try again. They make a hole, a silver tube. I glide right through and end up on the outside. They seal the hole back up.

I try to keep pace with them on the outside. My hair blows over my goggles. They move faster, tighter.

They don't look at me. I stop swimming. 'What?' I say. 'What do you want?'

They stop.

There's a kind of murmuring that rises up and around, a wall of noise. I can't make out anything. They cock their heads, look at each other and stop. A group gets nosed out of the shoal.

The others poke them in the back. They make an arrow, but it keeps changing. No one wants to be at the front, to stand out, everyone keeps backing off.

The one in the front gets nudged to keep going. It's Bob. I know it is by the way he doesn't look at me.

He swims close. Push, push, push. The others move him on. I want to grab him and get out of here.

He stops by my nose.

'*Stay*,' he says.

Stay

He looks back at the shoal. They move up, closer like a wall that's moving in, closer like a game of Grandma's footsteps. He swims up to my chest and darts between the tags and my body. I try and swat him away.

'No,' I say, shaking my head. 'No.'

Stay, say the fish. All of them.

Stay

Stay

I think of falling out with Dad. Of Mum's face in the kitchen. Of the wheelchair. It feels good to be wanted.

Bob swims in front of me. His eyes are big and hopeful.

Us

He says.

Us

He wants me to be part of the *Us*.

I shake my head. I can't stay.

He takes my tag chain between his teeth and swims up.

No Pink-fish

NO Patrick

No

He says.

A fish comes at me from behind.

No, it says and grabs the chain.
Another's by my side,
Another's by my neck.

No, they chant.

All of them are going for the chain. Like it's keeping me from them, in the *big-shine*.

I grab the metal. It's thin and digs into my fingers. 'No,' I say and kick them away. But they keep coming, breaking off from the shoal, more and more in a swarm, their bodies flicking up and around, closer, closer, closer.

No Patrick

No Pink-fish

Stay

They swim by my face. I can't see anything. They're strong, all together, they're really strong.

Stay

They say.

Stay

The chain's rising. I pull it down. My fingers are slipping. The metal's straining, I think it might snap, but it doesn't. It lifts. The water thrashes. I'm losing my grip.

I close my eyes. It's so hard to focus, to think. My head is full of fuzz. I squeeze my eyes shut to block out the fish froth. A tail whacks me in the ear.

Stay

They're lifting the tags over my head. Their tails push me down. I think of Mum being ill forever. Of Dad's angry face, I think about Jamie Watts and school and my fingers slip off.

Then I think about Zadie and that downhill bike ride feeling and Patrick. I picture his face, like he is bobbing in front of me. Like he is knocking on the front of my goggles. He is mouthing something. '*Megallas*,' he says all slowly in his silent goldfish face.

I open my eyes. '*Megallas*,' I say. '*Megallas, Megallas*.

STOP.'

BHAM.

The fish scatter like glitter tipped out in the sink.

I rise like a balloon, kicking for up and pop the surface.

I take a lungful of air and reach for my chest. The tags are gone.

Too Strong

I'm bobbing on the surface and gasping for breath. The wind stings into my ears. I feel the empty space on my chest. *It doesn't matter*, I think. I try to tell myself, *It doesn't matter, I'm out now.* But it does. Those tags were my escape route.

I feel my heart, like the water, thumping. It takes over my head. I look around. It's dark. Just a line of moon on waves, like a pathway, like a guiding light. I look for the shore but I can't see anything. I spin round and round. I don't know where I am.

I think of the orchid mantis. When it's born it has twenty minutes to harden its body under a leaf and pick a path. Left or right? Right. It escapes a jumping spider and gets eaten by another mantis. Mantis will eat anything that moves. Survival is just a matter of chance.

If I go the wrong way I'll be swimming out not in. If I go left or right I'll be swimming round forever. Three wrong ways, only one right one. I have no idea which one to pick. I don't know what to do. I bob up and down in the swell. It's getting higher. The water is throbbing. It goes through all of me, fills my ears, everything, it's too much.

My head goes under. I come back up, gulp air in. I don't know what to do. I try to fight back, to swim in. A wave pushes me further out. I think of Patrick. *What if you don't come back?* I feel cold. A chill that creeps up and into my bones. *What if you can't? What if you can't?*

I stop kicking. Killer whales chase the humpback calf and its mother till they're exhausted. Till the calf can't take it any more. The mother pushes him up on to her back to breathe and they move in for the kill. I think of giving up.

A wave gets my head from behind; my chin smashes down into my chest and hits something hard. The whistle, right. The water pushes me back up. I press my hand against it. It seems tiny. It seems stupid. But it's still a chance. I pull the whistle up and out of the suit. A wave hits and nearly pulls it out of my hands and over my head. But I hold on. My fingers are freezing – the warmth of the metal stings them awake. I grab it in my fist and blow.

The noise is sharp. It cuts into my ears. The sea tries to drown me out, but it can't. The pitch is too high. It cuts through and across and up and up, like it's lifting me out. I blow till my lips sting.

My head buzzes. The water throbs and growls.

Something is pecking at my foot. It nudges and strokes my neck. It whispers in my ear.

'*Growl*,' it says.

Growl

It sounds scared. It pecks me on the ear and scoots off.

I drop the whistle and close my eyes.

Banned

Two hands grab my shoulders and roll me up in a net. They haul me in, like a fish and lift me out. I feel the throbbing and realise that it's an engine, not in my head. I see the orange base, the inflatable edge and realise that I'm in a lifeboat. The boat is the *growl*.

A guy with no hair is steering, hood up, talking into the radio. Another straps a life jacket round my chest, a silver blanket over my head. 'Billy Shiel?' he says. I nod. 'Was it just you out there, son?'

I nod again.

'A laddie gave us a call,' the man with the radio says. 'An anonymous caller. You're a lucky one, eh.'

'It's Col you want to thank,' the blanket guy says and nods at someone on the other side of the boat.

'Ears of a bat,' the guy with the radio says.

Col says nothing, just walks over, lifts the whistle round my neck and nods. He looks deep into my eyes, like there's something he can see. Something no one else can. We stare at each other.

The guy next to me nudges my arm and says, 'Good preparation, son.' I see his face reflected in the whistle. 'Life saver.' I wonder where Patrick is right now. I put it back down under my suit. I wonder where Bob is.

Col pulls a stack of emergency response cards out of his pocket. 'How long were you in the water?' he says. I shrug. He reads the questions and I answer. *Temperature, skin colour, breathing,* His words drift out with the roar of the engine.

I pass.

They stand down the ambulance on the radio.

The boat speeds us off, back to the shore.

I watch my water world drifting away.

When we get to the land I just want to go home. Alone. But they won't let me. At the boathouse we drink tea with sugar in tin mugs. I feel it slide down and spread out inside.

Col passes me the biscuits. I eat three. 'You've perked up,' he says and winks at the others. 'Let's take him home, lads, eh.'

We get in the back of a blue Land Rover and bump along over the cobbles and away. I look out the window and watch the moon bouncing on the waves as we go.

Sea-caller
    Sea-caller

It disappears behind the crocodile rocks. I feel like a rabbit in a cage.

When we get to my house I want to run.

*

The boat guys send me upstairs while they talk to Mum and Dad. I go in the shower, put on my polar fleece onesie and get into bed. I feel hot but not sleepy. The front door shuts and Mum and Dad come up. Their faces look flat and serious.

'A mile offshore?' Dad says. 'A mile?!' He slaps his hand on his leg. 'What on earth were you thinking?'

'It was okay,' I say. 'I was in control.' I look out the window.

'You weren't,' Mum says. 'You were lucky. Thank god someone was there.'

'Bloody stupid!' Dad moves his arms like he doesn't know where to put them next. One goes on his hip, one in his hair. 'As if we didn't have enough to worry about.'

Mum gives him a look. 'Don't ever do that again,' she says stroking my fringe.

'Too right he won't be doing it again,' Dad says. 'We can't trust yer, can we? That's the end of it. Right.' He brings his hand down like an axe. 'You're banned,' he says and goes out the door and slams it behind him. Mr Minnington at number 46 whacks the wall with a frying pan. He hates door-slamming.

Mum kisses my head. 'Get some sleep,' she says and goes out too.

I close my eyes and hear Mum and Dad arguing downstairs. I put my fingers in my ears and slide under the blanket like a snail into a shell.

Real Friends Talk

I get up and go to school. I'm a black rhino on the run. Full of fury.

Banned.

I wish Sir David was around. But he is nowhere. That channel has tuned right out.

At break I find Patrick in the usual place. I just stare at him. He stares right back. 'I've got your stuff,' he says and hands my tent over. It's all neatly packed up. I don't take it. It drops on the floor.

'Thanks,' I say. 'Thanks *a lot*.' I say a l-o-t really slowly. He looks confused. I don't know if he's stupid or just acting it. I pretend to pick up a phone. 'Oh yeah, hi,' I say. 'I'm an anonymous caller. I'd just like to ruin someone's life.'

He narrows his eyes. 'Repetitive breath-holding causes serious *brain* injury,' he says.

I turn around to see Joel and Becky staring at us. We walk over to the far end of the field, by the old chestnut where someone has turned RABIES into JELLY BABIES. I wonder if it was Mr Royston, the caretaker taking care of the tree. Wanting people to like it again.

'You were down there for ages,' he says.

'So?'

'So, I thought you needed help.'

'Well you thought wrong.' He didn't. I look at the floor.

'You were the one who asked me to go on lookout. I looked out, I couldn't see anything. It was totally dark. I couldn't even see where you were.'

'Yeah, well you won't be having to do that again,' I pull a strip of bark off the tree. 'I'm not allowed back in.' I curl the strip round my finger and pull it tight. 'Ever.'

'Oh,' he says. 'Sorry . . . I didn't think . . .'

'No. You didn't.'

'Actually I did. I kind of thought I didn't want you to die.' He pulls away, crosses his arms over his chest. 'What actually happened down there?' he says. 'What took you so long?'

I stare at the grass.

'Oh, so by the way.' He stares right at me. 'What's wrong with your mum?'

'Nothing.'

'Nothing?' Patrick keeps staring, like he's expecting me to say something else. 'I'm going,' he says and picks his bag up off the floor.

'Why?'

'I thought we were friends.'

'We were.' I'm totally confused. 'We are.'

'Real friends tell each other stuff. Real friends talk.'

'What's that supposed to mean?'

'I saw your mum.'

My blood freezes. 'When?'

'When you were down there, when I was covering for you.' He looks back, right at me. 'She went by. With your dad. In a wheelchair.'

I don't know what to say. I officially have nothing to say. So I say the most stupid thing, like saying it makes everything okay, like if I say it I can believe it. 'It wasn't her,' I say. 'It must have been someone else.'

'Grow up,' he says and turns and leaves. I watch him walking over the field, getting further and further away.

I scrunch my hands up into balls and shut my eyes. 'They asked me to stay,' I shout after him. 'Forever.' But the wind just carries the words off somewhere else.

Electronic Fog

On December 4th, 1970, Bruce Gernon was flying to Bimini when he saw a strange hovering cloud.

Bruce Gernon tried to fly over it but the cloud moved. It kept moving at the same speed as the plane and then faster until at 11,500 feet it formed a tunnel, dead ahead. There was no way of escaping it, so he flew in.

Inside the tunnel the cloud walls spun anticlockwise. The plane's compass and navigation tools went crazy and spun anticlockwise too.

Bruce Gernon flew on and out of the tunnel expecting some blue sky at the end. But there was none, everything was grey. He flew in the grey haze, seeing nothing, no land or sea or sky, not knowing where he was or where he was going.

The fog peeled away in ribbons. The compass stopped spinning. The Miami control tower gave him radar identification that he was directly over Miami Beach. He looked down and saw the beach. He looked again. It shouldn't be possible. A flight to Miami takes seventy-five minutes but he'd only been flying for forty-five.

I think of Bruce Gernon flying with no idea where he was going, what he was getting himself into. That what he thought was the right way was totally the wrong way, how the fog threw him off course, out of time, how his head was so muddled he had no idea where he was at.

The Eye of the Storm

After school I stomp home.
The cars go past like speedboats.

Growl

Growl

Growl

I nearly step out into one and get a *Hard-it* in the face.

But don't.

In my mind I walk through the Sahara Desert, miles and miles of heat and sand and emptiness, I fly up round the jagged edges of Krakatoa. I watch it explode. Thirteen thousand times the power of an atomic bomb. I think of the lava flooding out, boiling over, melted rock bubbling out of the earth. I pull up and out and into space like a satellite. I watch the storm coming, a white swirl on the thermal map, I watch it head for the Florida coast. Closer, closer, closer. I think of the people in the houses, the flats. The stuck ones, with nowhere to go.

I snap out of space and up our front steps.

I push the door open and head for the stairs.

'Where are you going?' Mum is standing at the bottom.

'Where do you think?' I try to push past her.

'Billy.'

'What?'

'Sit down,' she says.

'Why?'

'Because . . .' She slumps on to the step. 'Doctor Winsall came round,' she says.

'When?' I hear the wind rattling at the windows, pressing up against the house.

'When you were out.' She puts her hand on my shoulder. I shrug it off, watch the thermal camera, the white swirl shifting shape.

'They think they know what's wrong.' I swallow even though my mouth is dry. 'Well. They *do* know. They know what it is.'

The swirl gets up speed, comes closer, and closer . . .

She stands up and goes over to the dresser.

'I printed these.' She pulls out the drawer and gets out some papers. They say '*What is ME?*', '*Chronic Fatigue Syndrome – The Facts*' and '*Explaining the Inexplicable*'.

BOOM! The swirl hits the shore. The wind storms in, fists blazing, knocks over a bus shelter, pulls out a palm tree. Mum holds out a magazine cover with someone lying down in some leaves on the front. 'New Look, New Outlook!' it says. I don't want to look at them. I'm the crazy cameraman, the guy holding on to his balcony with both hands, locked into the storm. Staring at the sea.

'Do you want to read through one, together?'

'No,' I say and fold my arms.

She starts reading. I put my hands over my ears.

239

'I said no!'

I think of Sir David running for the shelter, locking himself into the bunker. In my head he holds a hand out, wild white hair blowing around his face. His hand looks good and strong. I want to take it. But I don't. I can't. I'm stuck, rooted to the spot.

'I don't want you to have a label like a . . .'

'A what?'

'A supermarket chicken. A dead chicken in a packet with a label on.'

'I'm not going to die. It doesn't say I'm going to die.' She reaches for my hand. I pull it away.

'They're just guessing,' I shout. 'It's just stupid guessing.'

The cyclone tucks me in its heart, wraps its wind arms around my chest, over my ears till I can't hear anything and everything fuzzes.

I run upstairs and slam my door. Mr Minnington bangs his pan.

I stick my face into my pillow.

Soft-it

Soft-it

Mum calls after me. 'It's not forever, Billy, it doesn't

say it's forever.'

She pushes a sheet under the door. I pick it up. There's lots of words, the only ones I see though are right at the top. 'There is no Cure for Chronic Fatigue Syndrome,' it says.

Sounds like forever to me.

The wind rattles the window. I shut my eyes. All I can hear is air sucking from one place to another, howling in my head, smashing up the world.

Then I see it.

A tsunami wave. Full of fish. Fish in the froth, in the foam, in the waves, in the spray.

Stay

They say, leaping into my face, bubbles popping out of their little mouths. I reach out.

Stay

All I want is to be there. Spinning with them again. Away from everything.

Stay

'Yes,' I say out loud. 'Okay,' I say and nod.

It sounds perfect.

The wind laughs its head off and leaves.

I open my eyes and blink hard.

The fish are gone.

Don't Worry

I get out a sheet of paper from the printer in the spare room and a black Rotring Fineliner out of Dad's don't-even-think-about-using-these box.

I take *How to Live With a Neurotic Dog* off the red metal bookshelf, as it is properly A4 size and lock myself in the bathroom. I sit on the black and white checked lino, my back against the bath. I look at the flying man, not flying. Waiting to fly. As if he's just looking for the right moment to shoot out of the window. To come alive. I look at the flamenco toilet roll holder. In my head I ask her for some advice. '*Que pasa?*' she says and stares right back at me.

The first line is easy enough.

Dear Mum and Dad,

The rest is trickier. I sit with the pen on the paper for a while and think. An ink blob leaks out and spreads. There's too much to say. I don't know where to start. So I write:

I have gone swimming. Sorry.
I might be a while. I don't know how long.
Don't worry about me. I will be okay. The fish will
look after me.
Love Billy

Then I draw a picture of a bean tin in the sea with fins and a tail, swimming under the waves. I prop the note up on my pillow, put my goggles round my neck and go downstairs. In the kitchen the clock sings like a snipe. I pick up the howling wolf towel, realise I don't need it and put it down again and head off out the back door.

Disappear

There's no one in at Zadie's. I look through the dried-out starfish section but there's just a big empty space where people should be. Maybe they've gone out like *normal* people do.

I walk down the cliff path. The sky gets dark. Slabs of cloud are hiding the sun. The wind blows them away and sends in reinforcements. Gravel digs into and between my toes. My skin is full of goosebumps.

When I reach the bottom the sand is cold and slaps under my feet.

I walk over to the water and stop. I wonder if Sir David's safe in the bunker, if he's come out yet. I look at the beach and think of rain frogs living under the ground. They stay there all year till it rains. Then the ground erupts. They all come out, find a mate and take them back down. Sometimes life is all about timing. Sometimes you know when the time is right.

I look up at the bone rocks. Chewed up and spat out in the water.

I've never been up there.

There's a sign that says 'DANGER: RISK OF EROSION' and a big black hand in a red circle. I look up at the ledge, at the crumbling, at the rock all chipped off and worn away. I look at the toe holes, the finger cracks, and I think, *I'm going up there*. I'm not wading in, not today. The time is right, I'm going to jump.

There's a hole in the middle of the bones, the sweet spot, the blood drip. If you jump off and hit that you're okay. If you miss it you're on the rocks, smashed up. Peter Rydon said he did it last summer, told everyone he did. Not that anyone saw.

The wind nudges into my back. *Go on then*, it says, *go on*.

I turn and walk over to the edge of the beach, to the base of the crocodile. I put my hand up the stones, feeling for a hold. I find a crack where the rock has split, jam my fingers in and haul myself up. My feet scrabble around, trying to find something to grip on to. They find a ledge, a thin one, I put them sideways to make the most of it and look for a new handhold. On the next pull up my hand slips and my elbow grazes and starts to bleed. I tighten my toes, grip into the gaps, keep my stomach flat, my body pressed against the face. I move up again. A shower of rocks slips down and smashes. My heart goes crazy. I walk my fingers over, on to the lip of the ledge. I don't look down. I put my other hand on. I pull my body up on to my elbows, breathe and pull again. My chest flops down on to the ledge and I swing my legs over. I look at my knees, the skin turned white. I look at the sky, the clouds turned purple.

I look around for Sir David but he says nothing, is nowhere.

I look down over the edge and think about barnacle geese. The only way to protect their young is to nest 400 feet up. On a cliff.

The chicks hatch and walk towards the edge.

The dad flies off and calls. They look down. They back off. They don't follow.

The mum tries, flies to the bottom. Cries out. They come closer to the edge. They can't fly, they won't be able to for another eight weeks. But there's no food at the top of the cliff.

They come closer to the edge. Closer. They have to jump.

The mum cries out again.

They follow. It's their mum. They have to.

The first one tips over the edge. Flaps its wings to slow its body down as it falls. If it hits a rock belly first it might survive.

I dunno.

The second one goes. It does better. Belly first. BHAM. It flips over. BHAM BHAM BHAM. It tips and flips all the way to the bottom. It doesn't move. Yet.

The third one goes. BHAM, tip, flip, BHAM.

It gets about halfway down.

The last one jumps. It's the best yet. A perfect drop. It BHAMs and crashes but it gets there, it makes it to the bottom and stands up and wobbles about, but it's okay. It's actually okay.

The one that wasn't moving gets up too. It looks wonky, but alive. It walks over to its mum. If they don't go now the foxes will come and eat the survivors. They have to move.

I look back over the edge. I just stand there, on the ledge. Breathing hard.

'Billy!'

I jump, but not down. I pull back and turn round. I see something. Someone. They're hunched up against the far side of the ledge, in a black sweatshirt, black jeans, black coat.

'Hey, Billy,' it says. Patrick. 'Ninety-eight per cent chance of storms. Didn't you check the forecast?' His face looks dark under the hood. It totally freaks me out.

'What do you want?'

'They want you to stay forever?' he says.

I didn't think he'd even heard that. I nearly fall off.

'You're crazy,' he says. I look at his eyebrows. *I thought you might need me but there's no way I'm going to say that,* they say.

The clouds are squeezing together, puffing up. The sea's not calm either. The tide's coming in. Waves smash on the shore, claw everything back, shells, stones, everything, then slam down again. In and out, over and over.

I think of Hurricane Katrina – so powerful it could power the whole electric grid of America, so wild it rips up one hundred miles of coastline.

I look down into the spray and see the fish tsunami, I see Jamie Watts's face like a killer whale opening up, rising out of the wave, I see Dr Winsall, I see *There is no cure.* I see Dad's head on the worktop, his tea towels

249

on the floor, Mum crying in bed, the wheelchair. I see her slipping away, fading, into something see-through, fading away into nothing. I see the coastline of Louisiana, Mississippi, Alabama, signposts pulled out of concrete smashing up windows, flood water rising, filling the streets. Cars bobbing upside down. I see the fish, the calm quiet nothingness. The way it feels to be there. One of them. Looked out for.

'Once they've got you, they won't let you go,' Patrick says. 'The fish.'

'They will,' I say. 'I'll come back. Later.'

'Did you see anyone else down there?' He gets up and starts walking over. He stands in front of me, his hair blasting from behind, covering his face. 'You'll sink. You'll drown.' He's shouting it against the storm. 'You'll just . . . disappear.'

The wind thumps its fists on my chest, into my back. *Go on*, it says, *go on go on*. There's a proper boom in the sky and a flash. We look up. For a minute it feels like the whole world shuts up. We're in the eye of the storm. The rain starts, hard and fast. Big drops, really big fat ones. I watch them bouncing off the white foam of the waves.

Patrick reaches into his pocket. I back off. 'What are you doing?'

'What does it look like?' he says and snaps a set of handcuffs over our wrists. 'If you're going down, you'll have to take me with you.'

Losing it

I look at Patrick. There's another flash, close, really close. So pure and bright it blinds me. When I open my eyes I see him wobble. His free arm swings round in circles while he tries to get his balance. He tips forwards. I reach out but it's too late.

We both fall.

Back and over we go. Down and down. Past the gulls' nests, past the peeling cliff edges, white stains running down the grey. I think of our heads landing on the bone rocks, splitting open. For a minute the wind seems to hold us, to lower us in its hands. I hold on to Patrick. I shut my eyes. I harden my back into a shell and get ready to break.

Smack. Our backs hit the water.

We hit the sweet spot.

I breathe out as we go down and the bubbles fizz around us.

Patrick totally freaks out, starts thrashing his arms and legs around. I grab him round the chest, like we did in life-saving class. I pull us up and get our heads out. He struggles as if I'm trying to drown him. Like he's scared out of his mind. I keep tight hold, even though I'm going under. 'Stop, stop it,' I shout when I can. I think of how a drowning person can pull a swimmer under, by the fright in them, by the panic. I keep hold of his chest and pull, kick away from the rocks. The water's in his coat and boots and trousers, dragging him down. I kick his boots off with my heels.

The waves get bigger. I hear them smashing on the rocks. I mistime one and get a mouthful of water. I choke with the salt but keep my head up, keep kicking. I feel how far the ground is beneath us. Gravity pulls us down. The tide pushes us back, as if it wants us out, like skin pushing out a splinter. It's trying to put us back on to the shore. I feel another boom and a flash straight after. The storm's bang overhead.

Patrick's so heavy he's slipping out of my arms. His legs kick. I try to keep his head up.

I pull right back, put my knee under him and try

to pull him out.

I can do this, I can do this, I can do this. I keep saying it in my head, over and over.

But I can't.

I feel like I'm losing it. I know I am.

Patrick's still thrashing.

We start to sink.

My head's going under and that's when I see them. Out of the gloom.

A long, silvery trail like a tentacle.

Coming straight for us.

For me.

Now or Never

I feel the first one under my back. Then another under my arm, then my neck, my foot, my head. I look down and see the shoal wrapping round us.

The water's thick with fish.

I twist my head to look at Patrick. He's stopped thrashing. His eyes are closed. His hair is flowing out, his legs and arms spread open. The water pulls and pushes us. A sandstorm blasts underneath. Pieces of ripped-up plant and rock and shell fly up and around.

Hard-it

They shout and split around the handcuff chain, then back in a loop to face it. Hundreds of eyes, staring. Confused. They poke my hand. They poke the chain. Bob looks at Patrick. Then back at me.

No-eyes

He says. The shoal pull back and shudder.

No-eyes

They think he's dead.
Sharks are the only fish with eyelids.
Bob looks at me as if he's passing on the bad news.
Pink-fish
Fast-dark
No-eyes
A *fast-dark* has pecked out *Patrick's* eyes.
He's sorry but that is how it is.
They swarm around Patrick. I keep hold of his hand.

No-eyes

No-eyes

They chant.

I look at Bob. He looks at Patrick. He looks at our hands.

No Patrick

No Pink-fish

No

Go

No

He says. The shoal looks at me.

Stay, they say

Stay

Stay

They start to push Patrick away.

'Stop!' I shout. But no one's listening.

The handcuffs start to stretch. Patrick drifts away.

FLASH

Lightning buzzes in the distance.

They stop. They stare at the light. My eyes get floaters.

Sea-caller

They say.
Sea-caller

Sea-caller

BOOM

The thunder hits.

The fish start up again. Push, push, push.

They push Patrick down.

I try to kick them away. 'No! No!'

They keep coming.

Hundreds of them.

Thousands.

Stay

Stay

They say. Altogether. They swarm round Patrick. They're so thick I can't even see his face anymore. I think of how brave he was. *Is*. That he came here to help me. He doesn't deserve this. SNAP. The handcuffs break like plastic. They push me backwards, out to sea.

'**No**,' I shake my head.

NO

I turn my back on them. I can't stay down here with them forever.

I've got to save Patrick. I swim over to him and reach out.

Flash

Pure white cracks through the whole of the sea. It's not a beam. It's a light bomb. They look terrified.

They pull back. I see Patrick. He's falling. Slowly. Down and down. Like a puppet with all its strings snapped off. I grab his hand and pull us up.

Soft-it, they say.

Soft-it

They want to hide.

We need to get out of here. We need to get to the shore.

'Go,' I say.

GO? Bob says.

'Go,' I say.

They look at each other. Head flick right. Head flick left.

GO, Bob says.

Go

Go, they say.

And we go.

Fast.

I feel slow and weak.

The fish aren't. They're flying.

They're muscle and bone, I think. Same as me. *Muscle and bone*. I say it in my head.

Muscle and bone

Muscle and bone
I am muscle and bone.

I feel the muscle stretch from my hip to my knee, from my knee to my ankle, from my ankle to my foot. I am a body that was born for this.

I feel my shoulders to my elbows, my elbows to my wrists, my wrist to my hands. I grab the water, hand straight, fingers curved. I pull it. Away from me. From us.

I am muscle and bone
I am muscle
and bone.

I kick through shadows and sea fog and blur.

Hard-it

We split through rock.

Soft-it

We dodge a current.

I'm too slow. It pushes me back.

I stretch out again.

Soft-it

I keep reaching.

Hard-it

I keep pulling.

We scrape over gravel and sea spit and sharpness.

I swipe it away with my hands.

Soft-it

We dive through sand smoke. It grits up my face.

Kick.

My legs ache.

Pull.

My arms are gonna snap.

Patrick's so heavy. I shuffle my hand around his chest. His ribs are sliding.

Kick, pull, kick.

Flash.

The light slices through.

I blink.

The water's thick and dark.

I have no idea where we are. The fish are slipping away.

I breaststroke kick.

I get a fingertip further.

I'm so slow.

The cold shark bites my stomach. I can't keep going. The fish flash pulls away.

My head is heavy. I think of me and Patrick sinking to the bottom.

Spinning.

Snowflake boys.

Twisting.

And landing.

And rotting.

And turning into bones.

And hag fish sliding in and out and picking us clean till we are white shiny skeletons.

Skeletons that sink into the sand.

And just disappear.

Patrick was right. We'll disappear.

The water pushes my hand off his ribs.

My brain is black and long and full of tunnels. I slip down one, into warm fuzzy easiness.

It's soft and flowing.

It's like a finger. A beam of light. Light like the moon.

It pulls me in.

Sea-caller

Sea-caller

Yes. I drift.

I float.

I drop.

And we fall.

Go

BOOM

Bob slaps me in the face. I open my eyes.

Fishy Boy?

They shut again.

No-eyes. No-eyes.

He nibbles my ear.
I try to swat him off.

BLAM

He whacks my nose.

OW

OW!

His bubbles lick my cheeks.

'Okay, okay.' I blink into the shine and look around. Everything is wobbly.

I look down. We're on the seabed, on the bottom.

I look up: burning silver. The *big-shine*. The surface is so close I could touch it. But I can't.

I'm stuck.

Patrick is on my back. My chin is in the sand. I try to get myself up on to my knees. I push my hands in and slip back down.

I need help. I need the *Us*.

'Us,' I mumble. A sand cloud blows out round the word. I hope Bob hears.

He swims off.

That's that then.

Never trust a mackerel.

I put my head down. Dirt grits into my eyebrows.

I shut my eyes, ready for the dark.

UP. Bob's back with pleady eyes.

UP, he shouts in my eardrum.

I look up and see them all. A shiny army. Small but strong.

The *Us*.

Hundreds of fish heads pile in. Thousands.

They nuzzle under my body.

UP, Bob says and they push.

They are a fish handy grabber.

The sand pulls down.

The seabed doesn't want to let us go.

We start to slide like a sucker on a window. Shells scrape under my stomach. *Come on*, I think, *come on*.

UP, Bob says.

UP, they say.

I pull up with my brain. I try to push with my arms and legs.

$$UP$$

UP

They heave. I push.
We start to move.

Nearly,

nearly,

nearly . . .

POP.
We ping off.
Sand swarms in under us.
Me and Patrick wobble on the fish heads.

Up, Bob says, *up*.

Up, I grin, up!
We keep lifting.
I think I'm gonna fall off but I don't.
I put my legs down. Patrick hangs off me in a piggyback in the air. His head's in the *big-shine*.

The rain stots on the top of my head. The wind bites my shoulders and the back of my neck. I keep my face under and look down.

The fish are squashed. It's dangerous for them here. They'll easily get pecked off by *fast-darks*. They're scared. They look at me, with eyes like sad dogs that want to leave but can't.

'*Soft-it*,' I say and flick my arm. I want them to be safe.

They need to go.

They don't.

Fishy Boy, they say.

Fishy Boy

Fish Boy

Fish

They won't split up the *Us*. They won't leave me. But they have to.

'*Soft-it*,' I say and point. '*Soft-it*.' There's another flash. They squeeze tight together.

Soft-it, they say.

Soft-it

Soft-it

They look at me, eyes raised. I nod. They turn and go. Looking for a kelp forest. For a safe place to hide the *Us*. All except one.

Bob stares at me. I stare back. The rain hisses.

'Go,' I say.

I don't want him to go.

I put my hand on my heart.

Ow? he says.

'Ow.' I nod.

We stare at each other. There's another flash. The sea turns neon. And then he's gone. Back to the *Us*. I lift Patrick up to stop him slipping off and step out into a new me.

Just an Illusion

I carry Patrick as far as I can and fall down on to the sand.

His eyes are still shut.

The rain drills into our heads.

I lie him down in the recovery position, like we learned in Heart Start. On his side, arm across his chest onto the sand. I say his name over and over. 'Patrick, Patrick,' I put my finger in his mouth. 'Wake up,' I say, 'wake up.' I move his tongue, clear his airway. Nothing.

I press on his chest. I blow in his mouth.

'Come on!' I slap his back.

A gush of water and sand spits out.

'You made my mouth full of sand.' His voice sounds slow and groggy, but alive. Definitely alive. It's a blummin' miracle. I jump on to him and hug him.

'Assault, assault,' he cough-yells. We roll over and over and when we stop I laugh a bonkers letting-it-all-go-ness.

We lie there on our backs with the water bouncing off our faces.

'What happened?' he says, choking up the salt.

'You don't want to know.'

'You saved me.'

'Nah, you saved me,' I say and look him in the eye. 'Thanks.'

He shrugs, wipes the rain off his face.

I look up at the sky. The clouds start blowing away, getting sucked out to sea.

It starts to ease off.

'How did you know I was going to be there? On the crocodile rock?'

'Magic's mainly about probabilities – it's all in the preparation,' he says. 'I knew you were gonna turn up, I just didn't know when.' He sits up. His sleeves droop over his hands. 'Pick a number between four and eight.'

'Not again.' I finger shoot myself in the head.

'I'm trying to show you something, okay.'

'Okay, okay!' I flop down on the beach. 'Five.' I don't even bother trying to work it out. Or working out how he will work it out.

He rolls up his sweatshirt. The water spurts on the

sand. *I knew you would pick five*, it says.

'*Surprise*,' I say all slowly and play dead.

'Get up,' he says and pokes me in the leg. 'Look under the other sleeve.'

'Why?'

'Just do it.' I roll over and wring it up. *I knew you would pick four*, it says. This actually is a surprise. I try to hide my eyebrows. 'Trousers,' he says.

'Seriously?'

He just points at the trousers. *I knew you would pick eight* is on his left leg. *I knew you would pick seven* is on the right. It seems so simple, so totally obvious. I have no idea why I never even thought of it at all. 'Preparation,' he says.

'When did you do that?'

'Before.' He buries his feet in the sand. 'Just in case.'

'You're crazy,' I say, 'in a good way,' and friendly punch his shoulder. I feel my chest, where my tags aren't any more. 'The fish took the tags,' I say. 'Sorry.'

'It's okay!' He waves a hand. 'Fish sense stuff.' He sits up with his hands holding his head. 'Catfish have over twenty-seven thousand taste buds on their body.'

'Actually most fish have taste buds all over their body. Seals can sense a fish trail from over six hundred metres awa—'

'And by the way. Fingers of steel . . .' he flexes his

274

fingers, 'SAS training. My dad's in the army. That's why we move all the time.'

'Oh.'

'You know why I learned magic,' he says. I shake my head. 'So people would like me.'

'Everybody likes you.'

'Not everybody.' He ducks his head down, so I can't see his face. 'I hate moving,' he says. 'I hate it.'

'Oh.' I am totally surprised. I think of how he always seems so happy, confident; how everything is all just an illusion, how eyebrows don't show everything. 'You should really learn how to swim,' I say, 'just in case you feel like disappearing forever.'

He sits back up and smiles and pushes me so hard my head bounces off a tide ridge and into a worm cast.

I pull him down with me and his head stots too.

We lie next to each other, staring up at the sky. It looks so big. I smile and my head drifts off and up. Although we're on land, it totally feels like we're flying.

Suddenly I see Sir David's face coming out of the clouds. I've missed him loads. I want to hug him. He's in his best blue shirt. He grins. 'Nature's greatest triumph begins with the leap of faith,' he says, 'flight. The extraordinary power to defy gravity that has shaped evolution and created a kingdom in the sky.'

Odd, but Okay

The rain has stopped. We sit up.

Patrick wipes the sand off his face. 'You'll see him tomorrow then,' he says.

'Who?'

'Bob.'

'I don't think so. Mackerel migrate in October.'

'He might come back though.'

'Maybe.'

'BILLY!'

I look up and see Mum and Dad at the top of the cliff, shouting. Mum gets up out of the wheelchair and starts coming down the steps. It's a struggle.

I run over to meet her. I don't want her to have to come any further. I put my wet face in her neck.

'Don't ever do that again.' She's half mad, half relieved. 'We read the letter. I thought you were . . .' she starts to cry. 'I love you,' she says and holds me so tight I can't breathe.

'It's all right Mum,' I say. 'It's okay.' I hold her right back.

Dad catches up. 'Never again, Billy,' he says, 'never.' He grips the two of us like a gecko.

Patrick comes over. He leaves a kind of slug trail across the sand. Mum wipes her eyes on her sleeves. She sees the broken handcuffs on our wrists. 'What on earth were you thinking of?'

'Harry Houdini,' I say.

'Billy was giving me a swimming lesson,' Patrick says. Mum stares at his clothes all hanging off him, his sweatshirt comes down to his knees. 'A life-saving one.'

'Well, that explains everything then,' she says.

'Patrick,' I say, feeling the new me rising up, 'this is my mum. She has ME.' Mum and Dad give each other a look and try to keep their eyebrows level.

'Oh,' Patrick says. 'My cousin had that.'

'Really?'

'Yeah, she's doing really well now though.' I give him a look that says *you never told me* and he gives me one back that says *you never asked*.

277

'So you found the creature from the black lagoon,' Dad says, trying to break up our looks. 'You can make a lot of money from that. Museums, tours, freak shows.'

'Dan!' Mum whacks him. He lifts her over his shoulder and runs off going 'Raaaaaa'.

At the top of the steps, Mum sits down in the chair and passes us towels she's brought just in case.

I wrap myself up and stand next to Dad. We look out over the railing. The sand, the sea, the bay, beyond. I think of Sir David in the Australian outback, by the Bungle Bungles. 'There's a story that unites each of us with every animal on the planet,' he says, 'it's a story of the greatest of all adventures. The journey through life.' A rock wallaby bounds off, wild and free.

Dad taps me on the head with a knuckle. 'Give you a fiver for whatever's going on in there,' he says and smiles. He puts his arm round my shoulder and leans in. His chest is hot and soft.

I brave up, feel the new me inside, all or nuffin. 'Dad, Jamie Watts stole my Nikes,' I say.

'I know,' he says.

'You know?'

'Yeah.' He winks. 'I just wanted you to tell me yourself.'

'Why?'

'So we could sort it out when you were ready,' he says. 'Has he been picking on you?'

I think of Ben's PE shorts, of how he hid Henry Atkinson's wind chimes, how he's had like ten detentions already. 'He's on white report,' I say, 'he kind of picks on everyone.'

'So what do you wanna do?' He puts a hand on my shoulder. 'You want to get them back?'

'No.' I shake my head and think of the sweatshops. 'You know people get paid nothing to make those,' I say. 'It's horrible. It's totally wrong.'

'True.'

'Anyway, I've got a plan,' I say.

'Okay.' Dad makes a hand into his *bang and blast* pistol. 'Hit me with it.'

*

On the way home the sun breaks through and shines over everything. Poking in and out the houses. Filling all the empty spaces. Dad asks if I want to take a turn pushing the wheelchair. It feels odd, but okay. We stop off at John's Corner Shop. 'Pay day,' Dad says and disappears inside.

Me and Patrick and Mum wait outside by the blue 'It Could Be You' lottery sign, by the steps. People walk past us into the shop. No one actually even notices us.

Then I see Jamie Watts from halfway up the street. He crosses the road, to our side.

My hands are sweating. I must do something. I have to do something. He looks so different away from the pack. On his own. He's got a Scottie dog with him on a lead. I think of Dad and Miso Angry. Sir David Attenborough says, 'In a threatening situation the male silverback will ferociously beat his chest and throw vegetation.' I have no vegetation. But I am not a mackerel. I'm not looking for a kelp forest, for safe ground.

Jamie gets nearer and nearer.

I count down the slabs.

Three . . .

I look at Patrick and put my hands to my chest. Elbows out, fists in. He looks back at me, over at Jamie. 'Silverback?' he says. I nod.

Two . . .

Patrick brings his fists up and we bang. Hard. Fists flying, chest pummelling. We are properly loud. A kid over the road puts his phone in his pocket and turns round. A bloke by the zebra crossing gets off his bike. Two guys with Curly Wurlys stop talking and stare.

One.

Face to face, eyeball to eyeball.

I look at Patrick and nod. We let him have it. We roar. Our voices come out and over and up and down and into the ears of the kid with the phone and down the throat of the bloke on the bike and in and out of all the gaps of the Curly Wurlys. Even Mum puts her hands over her ears. Enough, it says, is enough.

Jamie properly jumps. His dog barks. He looks around and tells it to shut up. It doesn't. He yanks the lead and it bites him on the leg.

We stop, ears ringing, throats sore. Jamie tries to look unfazed. He hobble-limps off down the street. Patrick looks over at me and we laugh so hard snot comes out of our noses.

Dad comes out of the shop with the biggest pile of Katzenzungen boxes you've ever seen. We're laughing like a pair of kookaburras. 'You okay?' he asks. He looks down the street at Jamie. Back at us.

Patrick looks at me. I look at Mum. Her eyebrows are happy surprised. We all look at Dad. 'Yeah,' I say. 'We're totally bonkers.' I wipe my nose with the back of my hand. 'We're okay.'

Dad winks at me and puts a hand on my shoulder. We stack the chocolates on Mum's knees and he races us down Kirton Street so fast Mum has to hold on to them with both hands and her chin.

When we get home, Me and Patrick have hot showers and I lend him my hand bison sweatshirt and black jeans. When we come downstairs Dad's got fish and chips in. The kitchen smells like heaven. I have scraps on mine and triple-load the salt and vinegar till it stings my gums.

'Blummin' lovely,' Dad says dipping a chip in curry sauce.

Mum shares out a jumbo sausage. 'Family tradition,' she says. 'Saves on the lip salve.'

'Doesn't it feel kind of weird?' Patrick leans over and points at my plate. 'Eating fish?'

'I'm a cannibal,' I say, licking my fingers and we eat until there's nothing left but papers.

After that, we go into the lounge and Dad plays all different songs with ME in. 'Rock With ME' and 'Won't You Take ME to a Funky Town' and 'Say a Little Prayer for ME' and we dance. I'm a pretty uncoordinated dancer. So is Patrick. None of us look at each other. We all just lose ourselves in what we're doing. The world seems to spin in a bright and brilliant way. Dad dances Mum in her wheelchair to 'Where's ME Jumper' by the Sultans of Ping FC and me and Patrick take our sweatshirts off and chuck them around. Mum goes to sit on the sofa with her head on the chameleon cushion, curls up and smiles. She drifts off while we keep dancing. Dad plays 'Close to ME' by The Cure. I love this song. I think of the video: they're all in this wardrobe that falls over the cliff into the sea, but they keep playing, even though they're sinking. I think of us as them. Bobbing around. I think of how we don't know when Mum's gonna get better, when things are gonna be okay, but now the secret's out of my chest I feel lighter, okay. Happy. I look at Patrick headbanging and for the first time in ages, I feel totally afloat.

Compass Malfunction

There's only two places on earth that make compasses point to True North instead of Magnetic North. The Bermuda Triangle and Devil's Island (off the coast of Japan). Some people say that this is what causes the problem, that this causes compass malfunction and sets the ships and planes off course.

But other people say that actually, navigators always compensate for magnetic declination when charting their courses and that calculation errors anywhere could cause anyone to go off course.

In other words, we still have no idea.

I think of how swallows have compasses in their heads, how that's kind of how we are too. Sometimes our heads see stuff the wrong way. Like the magnet is in wrong, flipped over. You think you're looking north when actually you're not. You've been looking south all along. If you turn yourself round and see it from the opposite way, everything looks different. Completely, utterly, totally different. In my head I ask the puffin on the Puffin Nuffin mug and he just eats a sardine and says, 'heavy man, heavy.'

Just the Beginning

This is the last thing I write in my *Unexplained Mysteries of the World* report. I walk to school in my new bright white Shoe Fayre trainers and put the report down on Mrs Ahira's desk. It looks pretty thick actually. 'Wow!' she says and lifts it up like it's a goblet from the lost city of Atlantis or something. She gives me two house plus cards and a student raffle ticket.

I go into class with my new reset-compass head on. Everything looks different. Like I've been pointing in the wrong direction the whole time. I think how we're all so scared of everything, of each other, scared of mucking up, scared of looking stupid, scared of being laughed at.

After art I actually *talk* to Ben Nicholson. It's

amazing how you can sit by someone and not know anything about them at all.

'Hi,' I say.

'Hi,' he says. His eyebrows look suspicious.

I look down at his desk and see he's drawing a Clone Trooper. He's just about to cover it up, when I say, 'That looks really cool.'

'Thanks,' he says, 'the angle of the head is a bit off.'

'Want to draw on my shoes?' I put my foot up on the desk.

'Really?'

'Yeah,' I say. 'Your drawings are amazing.'

'I'll have to do some sketches first,' he says. 'What do you want?'

'You're the artist,' I say.

He shrugs, 'I think we should go with the fish thing.'

Mr Neilson lets us use the art room at break and I sit with my feet on the desk.

'How long's it gonna take?'

'A while.'

It takes ages. First Ben does some paper sketches for scale and design possibilities. Then he draws on the shoes. Then he inks it in. I keep my feet in the shoes throughout the process. We tried taking them out, but it made the edges too squashy.

'Finished,' he says at last and stands back to squint at his work. They look totally amazing. Ben nods and half smiles. 'Not bad,' he says. I think how he must be the biggest perfectionist I know.

Everyone gets bright white Shoe Fayre trainers after that. Mr Neilson chucks us out of the art room after the first few days. Luckily the fall wall's just the right height for shoe sitting. Each of Ben's designs are unique, like the person wearing them. He draws the stuff that makes them different, the stuff that makes them them. They are mint.

The fall wall spot gets kind of busy. People just stay around to hang out together, even after their shoes are done. Harry, Shane, Todd, Leo, Alex, Sarah. Zadie. It feels strange but nice.

At the weekend I give Patrick his first actual swimming lesson and walk up to Zadie's house. I realise how this route isn't really any kind of shortcut at all. It's just the way I want to go. My magnetic north.

I see Zadie. Alone. She waves and sticks her face up to the feature window, next to the cockles, in her new bloodsucker shoes. She taps the glass. I go over. She opens the window.

'Nice shoes.'

'Cheers.' I look at the vampires on one, the werewolves on the other. Fur and blood drips and wings. 'I didn't want to pick y'know. They're actually enemies. Traditionally.'

'I'd pick the werewolves.'

'Yeah, but they can't fly,' she says.

'Vampires can't howl,' I say.

She shrugs. 'They can if they practise. A lot.'

'They're both good,' we say together.

She smiles and makes one shoe talk to the other. 'Peace?' say the vampires. 'Never,' say the werewolves.

'Shame,' I say.

'Yeah.'

She fiddles with her jeans. 'We're going out for Chinese for my birthday,' she says. 'D'you want to come?' For the first time I'm not the only person to go red.

In my mind Sir David points out the twelve-wired bird of paradise. 'Courtship appears to be some kind of game,' he says. The bird pole dances up and down a pole and pokes the female with its beak. I switch Sir David off.

'Okay,' I say, 'thanks.'

I poke my arm through the window and Zadie writes her phone number on the back of my hand.

'See you on Saturday.'

'Unless zombies take over the world,' she smiles.

'Okay, yeah.' We grin. 'Unless that happens.' I wave and go.

Once I'm past her house I practise walking as fast as a black spiny-tailed iguana. I move like the wind, like lightning, like the fastest no-shoes-and-reset-compass boy you've ever seen.

The Future

Me and Mum get the wheelchair out.

I fold down the sides and bump it down the steps.

Mum clicks the front door shut.

We look at each other.

'Ready?' I say. I stand at the back and hold the handles.

'I don't know.' She pulls a face. 'I've got more energy this morning,' she says, 'can't we just walk for a bit.' She looks at me and we both start laughing. She rolls her eyes and gets in.

We go to the end of the street. We turn right, turn left. I'm pretty good except for the curbs. An old lady in a purple coat comes up the street and grabs my arm. 'Strong as lampposts,' she says and whistles. She does a Tarzan and walks off again.

We stop when we get to the cliff path. It's too hard to push in the gravel. She takes the left handle, I take the right. We walk along looking at the empty chair, the empty space.

I look down.

'Mum . . .'

'Yeah.'

'I wish . . .'

'What?'

'I wish it would disappear.' I pick at the side of my finger. 'The ME. I don't want you to disappear.' She puts her arm around me and I lean into her chest and we stop.

'Listen,' she says. 'Can you hear it?'

'What?'

'Me.'

I listen. I hear her heart. BANG, BANG, BANG, it goes. BANG, BANG, BANG. 'I can hear it,' I say. 'I can hear you.'

'Good,' she says and holds me tight. 'Cos I'm still in here. Inside. Inside I'm ready, waiting, bursting to get back out again.' She breathes out. 'And I will,' she says. 'I will.'

She ruffles my hair. 'Shut your eyes,' she says.

'Why?'

'Dr Winsall says I have to do visualisation.'

'What's that?'

'Just shut your eyes.'

I check she shuts hers first and then I shut mine. 'What do you see?' she says.

I don't see anything. 'Nothing, darkness, black,' I say. I see the blood in my skin.

'Look harder,' she says, 'think harder.' We both just stand there. My body wobbles about. 'I see you,' she says. 'I see you and me at the beach. It's sunny and I've got my swimsuit on.'

'With the red spots?'

'Yeah, with the red spots. And you're wearing your sea slug trunks. Don't splash me,' she says, 'you're splashing me.'

'I'm not.'

'You are.'

'You started it,' I say.

She taps me with an elbow. 'Anyway I don't mind. It's okay cos I'm getting in the water.'

'Me too.'

'It's cold,' she says, 'but very, very blue.'

'Yeah.'

'And we're swimming together again. Like a pair of seals.'

'Like dolphins,' I say.

'And we swim out. To the crocodile rocks.'

'Past the crocodile rocks.'

'Okay. Past the crocodile rocks and back again,' she says. 'And Dad's got the towels ready.'

'And some hobnobs.' I feel the sunlight making my eyes all gold. I see us together, running, laughing. Dad pretends to chainsaw our heads off and we fall down dead in a big laughing pile on the sand.

'Mum . . .'

'Yeah.'

'I think we can open our eyes now.'

'Okay.' she says. 'Righto.'

And we open our eyes and we just stand there, looking out into the world, at all the things that might or might not happen. And it's okay.

Sometimes hamsters need to curl up in a big pile of sawdust, and meerkats bolt back down their hole, conger eels pull their heads back in the rock crack and monkey beetles lie down in daisies and let the petals curl up over their heads and hold them out of the cold, all through the night, till morning.

Life is full of *hard-its* and *soft-its*.

I am Fish Boy. My mind goes up and down like the waves. My thoughts go in and out like the sea. I am Fish Boy. I am me.

About ME . . .

In Britain about 250,000 people are affected by ME.
ME = Myalgic Encephalopathy.
People's symptoms are different.
It can mean: a total lack of energy, aching muscles,
that you're unable to concentrate, that you can't
sleep well.
Sometimes it happens after a bad illness, sometimes it
just happens.
There is no cure and no effective treatment.
It's still a bit of a mystery.

If you'd like to find out more, the action for ME
website www.afme.org.uk is a great place to start and
has lots of helpful information and links.

Fish Speak

Hard-it anything
hard – to be avoided

Soft-it anything soft – can be swum through

YES food – any kind

THIS? a suspicious feeling for
something that cannot be identified and
makes you stop

_OW_ OW

The suck the sky – the empty space
without water that pulls the life out of all fish

Fish Speak

Big-shine the surface of the sea

Fast-dark a mackerel-eating
bird – the shadow that comes from the sky
into the big-shine

Growl boats

No-eyes death

The Us the shoal

Sea-caller the moon

Pink-fish
Billy's made-up fish speak
for humans

Acknowledgements

There's a very fab David A fact about crows which didn't make it into the book but is this: 'In the city crows pick up nuts and drop them on zebra crossings. They let the cars crush the shells off and then hop along on the green man to eat the nut.'

I love this and it makes me think about books and writing.

Books are very hard nuts to crack.

I'd like to spend a bit of time if it's okay saying thanks to everyone that's helped me along the way and been a part of this. Hopefully we are all now happily dancing up and down on the green man.

Beep beep beep! Hooray!

Thank you:

Chris, Tom, Wilf, Twinks, Chang and the buzzard gang.

Pam Matthews.

Katie & Charlie Darby-Villis.

Richard Jones for putting his heart into these pictures.

David Almond for being a real inspiration and an all round lovely bloke.

The big shouldered & contagiously enthusiastic Mr Ben Illis and the wonderful BIA family. I'm so happy to be with you all!

The particular patience, kindness and care of Leah Thaxton, Naomi Colthurst, Natasha Brown, Lizzie Bishop, Emma Eldridge, Hannah Love & all the invaluable team at Faber.

Writing champions Claire Malcolm, Anna Disley & everyone at New Writing North. Plus the existence of the brilliant Northern Writers Awards! Fantastic!

The Newcastle University Creative Writing MA course and tutors, in particular: Ann Coburn, William Fiennes, Helen Limon, Sean O'Brien & Margaret Wilkinson. Plus the AHRC for their studentship. I wouldn't be here without you.

My university & Hexham writing gangs for the best support a person could want: Jill, Eleanor, Sue, Jamie, John, Annie H, Ian and Anouska. Debbie, Wendy, Sylvia, Berni and Margaret.

The sage genius & encouragement of Linda France.

To my lovelisome big sister and M&D.

My first ever writing teachers, the fab Penny Grennan and Janine Wood.

And all the other amazing people who've been there and given me a leg up or kindness or a hug I'm really sad that there isn't the space to fit you all in here but I hope you know who you are.

THANK YOU
all of you
in many many ways.